PROMISE YOU'LL
Stay

JULIANNE MACLEAN

PROMISE YOU'LL STAY
Copyright © 2016 Julianne MacLean

ISBN-13: 978-1-927675-48-9

Cover Design: The Killion Group, Inc.
Interior Formatting: Author E.M.S.

CHAPTER

One

Here we go again—entering a perfect stranger's intimate world...
Jocelyn Mackenzie followed her client out of the mahogany-paneled elevator and across the marble vestibule, to the double doors of the ritzy Chicago penthouse. She glanced up at the crystal chandelier overhead and the modern steel sculpture against the side wall, and felt the familiar sensation of wonder.

Not that she hadn't seen her share of fancy penthouses and stone mansions. To be honest, that's where she usually took assignments as an Executive Protection Professional, because quite simply, the average Joe couldn't afford her. It was for reasons of her own, however, that she would never choose this kind of lavish, pretentious lifestyle for herself.

The elevator doors slid closed behind them, and Dr. Reeves knocked on the door to the penthouse. Jocelyn waited beside him, hands at her sides, curious as to how Dr. Knight—her potential "principal"—would answer. Would he open the door without asking who it was, or would he use the optical viewer?

The crystal knob turned, the door swung open, and Jocelyn found herself gazing up at a darkly handsome gentleman dressed in a tuxedo, his starched, white shirt unbuttoned at the neck, his black bowtie undone and dangling in front.

He appeared to be in his early thirties and looked like he belonged on the cover of *GQ* magazine, which might explain why Jocelyn was here: This gorgeous, wealthy surgeon probably had more than his share of obsessed lovers and stalkers.

Dr. Knight's expression warmed at the sight of Dr. Reeves, then his eyes moved with interest to Jocelyn.

"Mark, what are you doing here?" he asked in a deep, husky voice while looking at Jocelyn, not Dr. Reeves.

There was an underlying sensuality in his tone as he took in her appearance in the vestibule—a tone that warned her right off the bat that he was a flirt.

Why wouldn't he be? Most women would probably fall at his feet for the pleasure of being the object of that smoldering gaze. But Jocelyn had no interest in flirting. She was here to do a job. Nothing more.

Besides, she'd never been the type to go all giddy and weak in the knees from a handsome man's attentions. And she knew a player when she saw one.

Still holding the door open, Dr. Knight backed up a step. "Come in."

Dr. Reeves gestured for Jocelyn to enter first. She stepped inside, her loafers hushed by the Persian rug as she took in the style of the penthouse—the marble floors, the Grecian columns and the sheer square-footage and height of the ceilings. Classical music played softly from the living room just ahead of her, where the lighting was dim and restful. A glass of red wine had been placed on the coffee table. An open, hard-covered book lay beside it.

Jocelyn glanced up at another enormous crystal chandelier over her head in the center of the foyer, then met Dr. Knight's gaze and held out her hand. "Good evening, sir. I'm Jocelyn Mackenzie."

He hesitated a moment, then shook it. "It's a pleasure to meet you." He looked over her shoulder at Dr. Reeves. "What's this all about?"

Jocelyn turned. Dr. Reeves—the man who had retained her services as Dr. Knight's bodyguard for the indeterminable future—fumbled for an answer. The two doctors stared at each other for a second or two.

Great.

"He's not expecting us?" she asked Dr. Reeves.

"Should I be?"

Jocelyn fought to suppress her annoyance. She didn't appreciate being misled, nor did she wish to work for anyone who wasn't absolutely in need of her services—and wanting, indisputably, to work with her. She had been under the impression that Dr. Knight was anxious for her to begin. His friend, Dr. Reeves, had told her about the intruder who had broken into this very penthouse a few nights ago, and the threatening letter that had come the next day.

She'd already done the advance breakdowns on Dr. Knight's parking garage, the hospital where he worked, and his regular route to and from. She'd hate to think she'd been wasting her time.

"Now, wait a second, let me explain," Dr. Reeves said.

"Explain what?" her principal replied.

Jocelyn shook her head and stared at the man who had hired her. "He's waiting, Dr. Reeves, and frankly so am I."

"What the hell's going on here?"

Dr. Reeves raised his hands. "Calm down, both of you. Donovan, I wanted you to meet Ms. Mackenzie before you said no."

"Said no to what?" His gaze raked up and down Jocelyn's petite frame, from her starched white shirt and brown blazer, down the length of her pants to her brown leather shoes. "Who *are* you?"

Jocelyn faced him squarely. "I've been hired to be your bodyguard, Dr. Knight, but I was under the impression you wanted one."

"A bodyguard? Mark, you had no right—"

"I had every right. You're my partner and I'm not about to lose you and have to cover all our patients while you're laid up or dead. I'd be on call 24-7, and that was never how we intended to run our practice." Dr. Reeves's cheeks colored. "Besides, I'm worried about you."

The two men stood in silence, as if neither was sure what to say to the other.

"Maybe I should leave," Jocelyn said. "You two can discuss this, and when you've got it figured out, you can call me, though I can't guarantee I'll be available." She turned to go, wishing she had taken Congressman Jenkin's request instead.

Dr. Reeves grabbed her arm as she tried to pass. "Ms. Mackenzie, please wait."

Jocelyn glanced down at his hand, tight around her elbow, and sent him a warning look.

He immediately released his grip.

"I apologize. But Dr. Knight needs your services, and his patients need him. Chicago can't afford to lose its best cardiovascular surgeon, nor can I lose a friend."

She shook her head. "It's his choice, not yours. I need cooperation from my clients. They have to be willing and eager to work with me and take the situation seriously. Without that kind of commitment from the people I work with, I walk."

She tried to leave again. Dr. Reeves followed her out into the vestibule. Jocelyn pressed the elevator button.

"Please, I'm begging you," Dr. Reeves said. "Stay and check things out. See what you can do for him."

"Why is it that *you're* the one out here begging me, and not him?" She gestured toward the open door of the penthouse, where Dr. Knight was still standing in the foyer, looking as relaxed as ever, watching.

"I can convince him." Dr. Reeves took a desperate step toward his friend. "Donovan, you need her. You can't put yourself in danger like this. Your patients need you and at the very least, your penthouse needs a new security system. The police don't have time to give your case the attention it needs, and I sure as hell am not going to lose any more sleep worrying about you."

"I'll change my locks."

"That's not enough. If this attacker is determined, he'll be back. Besides..." Dr. Reeves lowered his voice. "Think of the Counseling Center. You're almost there, buddy, and it means everything to you. You can't take these kinds of risks with your life, nor can you give the project what it needs if you're checking over your shoulder every five minutes. You need to finish what you started."

A long silence ensued. Jocelyn had the distinct impression that Dr. Reeves had touched a nerve with that Counseling Center argument, whatever that was about.

Jocelyn pressed the elevator button again, and Dr.

Reeves returned to her. "Please, Ms. Mackenzie, don't go."

"You should have discussed this with Dr. Knight before you called me out here and wasted my time. I have a long waiting list of people who need and want my help, and this is not—"

"How long a waiting list?" Dr. Knight asked, moving forward to stand in the open doorway. He leaned a broad shoulder against the doorjamb.

Both Jocelyn and Dr. Reeves faced him in silence.

He had way of halting a conversation just by entering into it, Jocelyn noticed as she stared at him in a studious kind of way. He certainly was good looking.

"Long enough," she replied.

"So you're that good?"

"She's the best," Dr. Reeves replied. "She used to be in the Secret Service. She has a list of references a mile long. Very *impressive* references, Donovan."

Dr. Knight stepped out of the doorway and sauntered leisurely toward her. "Why did you leave the Secret Service?" he asked. "You weren't fired, were you?"

Now he was insulting her. "No, I wasn't fired. The money's better in this racket."

Money, as it happened, was something she needed a great deal of at the moment.

He nodded. "I take it you know how to use that Glock." He glanced down at the gun she wore inside her jacket.

"I can drop you on your ass with it, Dr. Knight, and that's without pulling the trigger."

He inclined his head at her and said nothing for a moment. She guessed he was taking his turn at being studious.

The elevator dinged and the doors opened. No one

moved. Dr. Knight continued to gaze at her, waiting to see what she would do. For a moment or two, they all stood in the gleaming vestibule while the elevator waited.

Then the doors quietly closed, and the lighted buttons went dark.

Jocelyn sensed Dr. Reeves' heavy sigh of relief.

"I'd like to know how you work," Dr. Knight said. "Then I'll decide whether or not I can commit."

Jocelyn raised an eyebrow. She almost laughed. "I'm afraid it's going to be the other way around, Dr. Knight. *I'll* be the one to ask the questions, then *I'll* decide if I want to commit."

To her surprise, Dr. Knight smiled at Dr. Reeves. "You've checked out her references?"

"Of course."

"Good, because I think I like her."

Dr. Reeves sighed again. "I figured you would."

J ocelyn leaned forward in the plush, white, overstuffed armchair and booted up her laptop. "So you think the intruder had a key, Dr. Knight?"

"Yes. He was already inside when I returned home from the opera three nights ago, and the door was locked as usual when I came in. He must have wanted me to think everything was normal, so he'd have the element of surprise on his side."

Dr. Knight crossed one long leg over the other and took a sip of his red wine.

"Possibly," Jocelyn replied as she typed the details into his file.

"And call me Donovan."

Jocelyn didn't glance up. She merely nodded. "Is that how you got that mark on your knuckle?"

Donovan looked down at the small scar. "You're very observant, Ms. Mackenzie. Yes. I got in a few good swings before he gave up whatever he was looking for and took off."

"And what do *you* think he was looking for?"

He shrugged. "That night, the police concluded it was a burglary. They said keys can be stolen easily enough, an imprint made in a matter of minutes. I've often left my keys in my lab coat pocket at the hospital while I grab a bite to eat, or I've misplaced them every so often."

"Doesn't everyone?" Dr. Reeves offered helpfully.

Jocelyn didn't crack a smile. "I don't. And if I take this case, Dr. Knight, the first thing I'm going to do is work on getting you out of habits like those."

Donovan's brow furrowed. "You've *never* lost your keys?"

"Not since I was in high school."

"You've never left your purse anywhere? Forgotten a credit card in a store?"

"Never."

Donovan set his wineglass down on the mahogany end table. "You must be a detail-oriented person."

"I'm an *everything* person. I value my security."

"Hence your career choice." He gave her a probing look that told her he wanted to know more about her career choice and why she was what she was.

Jocelyn returned her attention to her laptop. She wasn't about to give him the how's and why's of her life. She had her reasons, and they were her own. Besides that, she made it a rule not to divulge personal things about herself that cultivated a familiarity with her clients. She asked *them* the questions. It was entirely a one-way street, and it was best that way.

"Dr. Reeves told me a threatening letter arrived the next day," she said.

"Yes, the police have it. It said, 'You deserve to die.'"

"Do you have any enemies, Dr. Knight?"

"Not that I can think of. And call me Donovan."

"Any medical malpractice suits against you? In the past or pending?"

"No."

"And it was definitely a man who attacked you? You're certain of that, even though the intruder wore a ski mask?"

"I'm sure. Why? You look like you don't believe it."

Not the least bit concerned with what he thought she believed or didn't believe, Jocelyn continued to take notes. "I like to ask questions, Dr. Knight. Cover everything."

"Donovan," he repeated more forcefully. "Do you have a problem with first names?"

She stopped her note taking and looked directly at him. All she could think was...*perfection.* She wasn't sure if she'd ever met anyone so good looking in real life.

"I don't have any problem with first names, Dr. Knight. Do you have a problem with *last* names?"

He watched her for a moment, then the tension in his face broke, and he smiled—a friendly, almost playful smile. His eyes flashed and he exuded an impossible-to-deny charisma.

Jocelyn clenched her jaw and worked hard to ignore her awareness of him as a man, because she wasn't the flirty type. She was here to do a job, she had no interest in anything else, and she didn't like distractions.

He took another sip of wine.

Jocelyn turned her attention to Donovan's partner. "Dr. Reeves, do you know of anyone who would want to hurt Dr. Knight?"

He shook his head. "No, but it could be anyone. Donovan has a lot of...female acquaintances."

Ah. This was not surprising.

Jocelyn nodded. "Perhaps the man was a jealous lover or a husband of one of Dr. Knight's 'acquaintances?'" She turned back to Donovan. "Have you had any threats or meetings with anyone who would fit that profile?"

He held up a hand. "Wait a second here. I don't have *that* many female acquaintances, and certainly not ones with husbands, jealous or otherwise. Mark, you're making me out to be some kind of sex addict."

"Not at all," Dr. Reeves replied innocently. "I just want to make sure we have all the bases covered."

Jocelyn interrupted and spoke in a calm, professional voice. "I'm not judging you, Dr. Knight. To tell you the truth, I don't really care if you're a sex addict or a gigolo or a Chippendales model on the weekends for that matter. I just want to know who would want to break into your home, and what we might be up against, and how I can prevent it from happening again. Now, I would appreciate it if you would just answer my questions honestly and don't worry about what I think of you."

He set down his wineglass. Looking almost amused, he inclined his head at her. "I truly believe you *don't* care if I'm a surgeon or a gigolo, Ms. Mackenzie, and that, oddly enough, is what makes me want to hire you."

What did he mean by that?

He glanced at Dr. Reeves. "You chose well, Mark. Even if I didn't ask for your help."

"I knew you'd see the light," Reeves replied.

Donovan stood. "I'd like you to start right away, Ms. Mackenzie. Tonight as a matter of fact."

Jocelyn raised her eyebrow at him. "When I start—*if* I start—is entirely up to me. I'll take a look around and ask some more questions first, then, and only then, will I consider taking your case. So you might as well sit back down and think back to every woman you've been with over the past six months. Then we'll talk about a retainer."

Dr. Knight smiled again, and quite agreeably sat down.

⁓☺

She was the rudest, coldest, least friendly woman he had encountered since he'd finished medical school ten years ago. And she was completely irresistible.

After Mark left, Donovan followed Jocelyn into his bedroom while she examined the door that led out onto the rooftop terrace. She tried to stick a finger into the gap between the door and the frame.

"This needs to be reinforced. It should be less than one-sixteenth of an inch, or a pry bar could be slipped in and the door worked open. And you could use some more floodlights on your terrace." She tapped the glass. "Is this shatterproof?"

He nodded, and listened attentively to all her comments and suggestions, all the while thinking about how long it had been since a woman had spoken to him with such disinterest.

Because of his profession and his wealth—a good deal of which was inherited from his parents—women pasted on exaggerated smiles and laughed a little too long at his jokes. They generally dressed to kill, showing off cleavage and wearing spiky heels and glittery lipstick when they were in his company. The women in his life were predictable. They always had that "Maybe I can be the future Mrs. Dr. Knight" look in their eyes. Over the past few years, that kind of social life had begun to grow tiresome.

Jocelyn Mackenzie was different, however. She wore a plain brown suit with flat shoes, and practically no makeup. Not that she needed any. Her face had a natural beauty with healthy, rosy cheeks, full, moist lips, and big brown eyes a man could lose himself in.

She didn't give him that flirtatious look, either, batting her eyelashes at him. Hell, she barely even noticed him. She was more interested in the nooks and crannies of his penthouse where there were flaws in the security, and figuring out how best to fix those flaws. She didn't want to impress him. She didn't care if she pissed him off.

It was a refreshing change, for sure.

"So tell me, Ms. Mackenzie, is my penthouse in bad shape, security-wise?"

She glanced around the bedroom, her face serious, her gaze going everywhere. She eyed the mahogany, king-size bed and the cream-colored, down-filled duvet, the black-and-white photographs on the wall; she glanced at his dresser with his wallet lying open on top of it, loose change from his pockets scattered all around.

"There's always room for improvement," she replied, still in that disinterested tone. She moved to the door, wiggled the doorknob and tried the lock.

"You're being vague, now. Are you going to transform me, or not?"

She turned around to touch and inspect the doorjamb. "I don't transform people."

"No, but you said you were going to break me of some bad habits."

She gave him an unimpressed look. "Like leaving your keys places. If you leave the toilet seat up, that's your problem."

He followed her out to the kitchen. She glanced quickly at the stainless steel appliances, the butcher's block and the white custom cabinetry.

He would have given his eyeteeth to know what she was thinking. He could see the wheels turning in her head as she sized up his penthouse before she decided whether or not she wanted to take his case.

"Do you have any hired help?" she asked.

"Yes, I have a housekeeper who comes in every morning through the week."

Jocelyn walked down the hall and returned to the foyer, then faced him. She was petite, but there was a strength in her that she emitted like perfume. He wondered what kind of personal life she led. He glanced down at her hands. There was no wedding ring.

Some deep male instinct in him rejoiced.

"First of all, whether we work together or not," she said, "I would recommend updating your alarm system. The one you have is at least fifteen years old. It's a dinosaur."

"Done."

"And you need to *use* the system. Half the people who have them installed can't be bothered to punch in the codes, so they leave them inactive."

Donovan smiled. "I'm guilty of that, I'm afraid."

"I figured you were." She moved to the front door to gaze out the peephole. "Are you looking for round-the-clock management and surveillance, Dr. Knight, or just improvements to your home security?"

"I think Mark had a round-the-clock bodyguard in mind."

She faced him. "I asked what *you* wanted, Dr. Knight."

He thought about the baseball bat under his bed, and

how he'd stared at the ceiling for six hours last night, then fallen asleep on his lunch hour today.

Then he thought about what it might be like to have a twenty-four-hour-a-day bodyguard invading his life. Always nearby. *This* bodyguard, in particular.

"I think round-the-clock management might be beneficial—at least for the short term."

She nodded, then quietly returned to the living room. Touching a long slender finger to the book he was reading that lay open on the coffee table, she raised her eyebrows as she gazed over the page. "Triathlons."

"You look surprised."

She shrugged. "I was expecting it to be about art history or something. Do you compete?"

"Not these days. I'm just training."

She moved across the room and knelt on the white sofa, to pull the ivory-colored shears back to examine the windows.

Donovan watched her reflection in the clean, dark windowpane. She flicked a latch.

As she reached up to try a higher latch, her jacket lifted and pulled tight around her shoulder blades, and he could see that she had a shapely behind, trim and fit beneath her loose, wool dress pants. He suspected she was athletic. Probably a runner.

"I'm not much interested in art history," he said distractedly, watching her return to her feet and smooth out her clothes.

She ignored him, and that intrigued him even more. He caught a whiff of her long brown hair as she strode by him, which was pulled back in a ponytail, and he guessed she used green apple-scented shampoo.

A few minutes later, they were back in the foyer and she was reaching into her breast pocket for a business card. She gazed directly into his eyes. "You are *definitely* in need of help."

She handed him the card, and turned to the door.

He glanced down at the card, then followed her out to the elevator. "Wait a second. Does this mean you're taking the job?"

She pushed the button. "Yes."

"But...when will you start?"

The elevator dinged and the doors opened. She stepped inside. "Right away."

He felt a little flustered. "But how will we do this? If you're going to be my bodyguard, shouldn't you be staying here? Where are you going?"

As she pushed the down button inside the elevator, a tiny infectious grin sneaked across her lips. "I liked the look of those feathery pillows in your guest room, Dr. Knight, so if you must know, I'm going to get my toothbrush and jammies."

The doors closed in front of Donovan's face.

He stood blinking in the vestibule holding her card, feeling wildly exuberant, and totally surprised by the fact that his cool, reserved bodyguard actually had a sense of humor. And she was darn pretty.

Things were definitely going to get interesting around here.

Jocelyn grabbed hold of the brass handrail in the elevator, then tipped her head back and tapped it three times, hard against the oak-paneled wall.

What in the world had possessed her to say such a stupid, suggestive thing? She was a professional, and she had a well-deserved reputation for objective, serious behavior and an almost masculine demeanor that demanded respect from the world of executive protection. She *never* smiled at clients. Not unless they made a joke and etiquette required it. Never was *she* the one to make the joke. And certainly not a sexual one!

She reached the bottom floor and stepped off the elevator into the lobby. The uniformed gentleman at the security desk nodded at her as she passed by.

A few minutes later, she was walking down the dark street to where her car was parked, debating whether or not she should have taken this job. She didn't approve of rich, snobby doctors—especially gorgeous ones who wore tuxedos and went to the opera and ballet just to add polish to their appearance, and expected every female within spitting distance to dissolve into a puddle of infatuation at their feet.

It was all so pretentious, and she hated that kind of thing. She had her reasons, of course. And okay, maybe they were personal, but what happened in her life *happened*, and she'd experienced firsthand the kind of shallow pomposity people like Dr. Knight were capable of. She knew all about the social-climbing doctor type. The type who went to medical school just to get a summer home in the Hamptons, a yacht moored at the most prestigious club in town, and a Mercedes or two parked in a three-car garage.

A Mercedes. All through medical school, Tom had talked about getting one. He'd lovingly referred to his future purchase as "The Merk."

Jocelyn pushed those memories aside and pulled out her cell phone. She called her assistant, Tess, to tell her she'd be taking the assignment. She then retrieved her overnight bag from the trunk of her car, and headed back to Dr. Knight's high-rise, wondering if it wasn't too late to back out, and how she could go about doing that. Because despite everything she'd just told herself about how much she hated pretentious men who wielded their wealth like swords dipped in liquid aphrodisiac, she had responded to the bold, confident look in Dr. Knight's eyes just now. The sheer perfection of his face and his sexy swagger as he'd followed her around his penthouse, so relaxed and casual about everything, had made her feel uncomfortably warm beneath her starchy, cotton blouse. She'd had to work hard to keep her eyes to herself and concentrate on her job, and she wasn't used to distractions like that.

Perhaps she should tell him that her assistant just called

to inform her that her previous principal wanted her to return for another month.

But that would be lying, and she really hated people who lied.

Surely she could handle this.

Deciding to at least give Dr. Knight's case some time—it would be a hefty paycheck after all, and she really wanted to cover her sister's college tuition—Jocelyn returned to his building and purposefully didn't stop at the security desk to check in.

The guard didn't say a word. Sure, he might have already seen her come and go once, but that wasn't good enough for her.

She pulled out her phone and made note of it, then while she rode the elevator up, checked the red emergency phone, just to make sure it worked.

~ℰ

Donovan leaned back against the kitchen counter and sipped his beer. What had he been thinking, hiring a woman on the spot to move into his place and be his bodyguard? His *bodyguard*!

He should have given it more thought. He usually didn't make decisions on the spur of the moment, unless they were medical emergencies and circumstances demanded it. When it came to his personal life, he preferred to take three days to mull over a decision, just to make sure he wasn't acting impulsively.

Which in this case, he most definitely was.

Damn Mark for bringing up the Counseling Center. Mark knew Donovan too well. He knew he wouldn't be able to say no after that, because the Center was the most important thing in his life these days, and he wanted to see it through to the end. A security expert was definitely a sensible idea.

Sensible indeed. While his "expert" had been wandering around the penthouse poking her nose everywhere, all he'd been able to think about was what she might look like naked.

Unfortunately, that last bit weighed a little too heavily in the decision-making process. What could he say? He was a red-blooded man, and the idea of sharing his penthouse with an attractive woman who didn't seem to *want* something from him was an appealing notion.

To give himself credit, though, he supposed his decision was something his gut had played a part in. Somehow he'd sensed that Jocelyn Mackenzie was knowledgeable about security and more than capable, and for reasons he couldn't quite explain, he felt comfortable trusting her—which was a novel concept for Donovan.

The doorbell rang, and he carried his beer with him to answer it.

"That's the second time you did that," Jocelyn said as soon as their eyes met.

"Did what?"

"You opened the door without using the optical viewer."

"The peephole? I knew it was you."

"How?"

"I knew you were coming right back." He stepped aside to invite her in.

"I could have been anybody. And your security guard downstairs isn't a hundred percent reliable, by the way. I'll deal with that tomorrow, after a few more tests."

"Tests? What kind of tests?"

"I'm just going to see how easy it is to get by." With a large, black tote bag slung over her shoulder, she waited in the center of the foyer while Donovan closed the door.

"How do you *know* I didn't use the optical viewer?"

"I know. I heard your footsteps and there wasn't time. Lock that, will you?"

He stared at her a moment, then realized she was right. He hadn't locked his door, and if she hadn't mentioned it, he might not have realized it until he went to bed, when he made a point to routinely check locks.

Her brown-eyed gaze swept the penthouse again. "One of the first things I like to do is get a feel for the boundaries with new clients. Some people like their privacy and don't want me to disturb their things, or they want me to stay out of certain rooms. Other people want me anywhere and everywhere, attached to their hip so to speak. What about you, Dr. Knight? Any preferences? Limits?"

He considered it. Attached at the hip sounded kind of interesting, though he could imagine some other places he might prefer to be attached.

"Not really. Go ahead and snoop around, especially if you think it will help you do your job. You can go through my underwear drawer if it turns your crank."

She glanced at him, stone-sober. No giggles. No leaping on an opportunity.

This was new territory for sure.

"The guest room is down here," he told her, leading the way down the hall, fully aware that she knew exactly where it was. "You know, I've never done this before and I'm not sure how to treat you. Like a guest, or an employee?"

"I'm neither. Mostly, treat me like I'm invisible. I'll take care of myself and try to stay out of your way as much as possible. We'll go over the contract tomorrow, and I can fill you in more on how I work. I'll also need your signature to accept the terms. But it's late now, so…"

Donovan reached the door of the guest bedroom and held out his hand for her to enter first. As her tiny body brushed by his in the doorway, he breathed in the scent of her ponytail again. It smelled fruity, and the fragrance wafted by him and disappeared all too quickly, leaving him feeling a little parched, so to speak.

She glanced at the beer bottle in his hand. "What happened to the red wine in the fancy crystal glass?"

"My mood changed. You want one?"

She moved all the way into the room and set her bag on the bed. "No, I never drink on duty. So, you like Canadian beer?"

He looked down at the label. God, she was observant. "Yeah."

"Me, too. I didn't take you for a beer drinker, though." She unzipped her bag, pulled out a baby monitor and an alarm clock, which she set on the bedside table.

"That's two things then," he said.

"I beg your pardon?"

"Two things that have surprised you about me. Triathlons and beer."

She smiled noncommittally. "Yeah. Two things." She pulled out her laptop and set it on the bed, then unraveled the power cord and went looking for an outlet.

Donovan continued to stand in the doorway. "Can I get you anything? Towels? Something to eat? If you don't want a beer, there's orange juice and Perrier and Coke and…I think there's ginger ale—"

"I'm fine. If I want anything, I'll help myself if that's okay."

"Sure." He continued to stand there while she plugged in her computer at the desk.

After a moment, she approached him. "Look, you don't have to baby-sit me. It's my job to baby-sit *you*. I don't sleep much, so I'll be working late on some proposals for improvements to your alarm system, and making sure your place isn't bugged. I've got keen ears, and when I do sleep, I generally do it with one eye open, so you can relax and get a good night's sleep tonight, and don't worry so much about being able to reach that baseball bat you've got stowed under your bed."

Donovan slowly blinked. She'd noticed the bat, too. And she wanted him out of her hair. He couldn't remember the last time a woman had told him to go away, and certainly not in a bedroom doorway at this time of the night.

He never imagined rejection could feel so damn good. And so damn frustrating. But there it was.

He was quite looking forward to waking up in the morning and sign on the dotted line.

Sometime after three in the morning, wearing her tank top and plaid pajama bottoms, Jocelyn e-mailed her assistant, Tess. She gave her instructions to contact the two alarm system companies she trusted for quotes, and to arrange for Dr. Knight's locks to be changed first thing in the morning. She then shut down her laptop and rubbed her burning eyes with the heels of her hands.

Dr. Knight seemed to prefer lamps that gave off dim,

golden lighting. Relaxing and romantic, yes, but not very practical. She should have had the overhead light on, rather than staring at that bright screen in the semidarkness.

She rose from her chair to take her empty water glass back to the kitchen. After rinsing it out in the spotless, gleaming sink, she still didn't feel much like going to sleep, so she decided to look around the penthouse a bit more. She wandered leisurely around the kitchen.

Dr. Knight certainly had an impressive collection of cookbooks. He had an entire floor-to-ceiling bookcase full of them, and they covered everything from vegetarian cooking to Indian food to chocolate and poultry. Did he like to cook for himself? she wondered, imagining those hands of his stirring chocolate batter, cracking a delicate egg.

Something inside her tingled pleasurably as her mind meandered around that idea, but when she caught herself veering off the path of professionalism, she shut her eyes and shook her head. She spent the next few minutes forcing herself to think about the penthouse, instead of the man who inhabited it.

Jocelyn made her way out into the main hall and walked slowly in her bare feet, checking out the paintings on the walls. Most of them were contemporary landscapes, with plenty of seascapes as well. Closer to the front door, there were more framed black-and-white photographs of old abandoned, dilapidated farm houses.

She peeked into Dr. Knight's exercise room and flicked on the light. He had a treadmill, a life cycle and a weight bench, and again, everything was shiny and clean. There wasn't a hint of clutter anywhere. She wondered how anyone could be so perfect all the time.

Where did he keep his junk? Did he even have any?

She crossed the room to check the window latches, even though she had already checked them a couple of hours ago, then realized with some uneasiness that she was overcompensating for something: a personal rather than professional interest in poking around. She had questions about the man down the hall, sleeping soundly in his bed for what must be the first time in days.

An image of Dr. Knight stretched out on that huge bed burned suddenly in her brain. Her vision had him sleeping in jockeys, but maybe he slept in boxers. Or maybe nothing at all.

Darn, she was doing it again. She willed herself to stop, and tried to remember her rule about not permitting herself to entertain any *personal* curiosities about her clients.

Not to mention the fact that Dr. Knight seemed like Tom in every way, and she had no business feeling curious about anyone who resembled her ex—people who derived their joy from living in lavish penthouses, wearing expensive tuxes and being spotted at the opera.

Then again, a few little things had made her wonder if there was more to Dr. Knight than what appeared on the surface. She liked that he'd seemed flustered by her presence.

She came to the cordless phone in a cradle near the front door, and since he'd told her she could go through his underwear drawer if she wanted to, she decided to listen to his messages. One never knew where clues about stalkers could emerge.

She pressed the TALK button, waited for the dial tone, then accessed the first message.

"Hi, Donovan, it's Eleanor. I had a great time last week. Just wondering how you're doing. Give me a call." *Beep.*

"Donovan, where were you the other night? I missed you, baby. Oh, it's Christine." *Beep.*

"Hi, gorgeous. Where've you been? Call me when you get a chance. I have tickets to *Die Tageszeiten* on Saturday night, and no one to go with." *Beep.*

There was one message from Dr. Reeves, then four more like the first—more women sounding desperate and needy, wondering why Donovan hadn't returned their calls.

Pitying those poor women, Jocelyn shook her head and slid back into security specialist mode. She returned to her computer to note the names of the women, and decided to ask Dr. Knight about them in the morning.

~*❧*~

At 5:45 a.m., the baby monitor that Jocelyn had positioned by the front door woke her instantly. She heard the sound of a key in the lock. She sat up and grabbed her gun.

Slipping out of bed without making a sound, she glided out of the room and made her way down the hall. A woman was sneaking in, quietly closing the door while she made an effort to be quiet. Before she had a chance to turn around, Jocelyn was behind her with the gun pointed at her head. "Hold it!"

The woman screamed and jumped.

"Put your hands on your head!" Jocelyn ordered. Dr. Knight's bedroom door flew open and he came hurling out. Jocelyn kept her eyes on the intruder. "Get back in your room, Dr. Knight."

"No, no, it's okay!" he said. "This is my housekeeper!"

Only then did Jocelyn feel her own heart racing and the searing sensation of adrenaline coursing through her veins.

She lowered her weapon. "I thought you said she came in the morning! It's 5:45 a.m."

"She likes to start early."

Jocelyn's shoulders went slack. "You could've told me! What was I supposed to think when someone sneaks into your penthouse at this hour?"

Dr. Knight moved toward the woman at the door. "I apologize, Mrs. Meinhard. I'm so sorry. This is Jocelyn Mackenzie. She's a security specialist. I hired her last night. Jocelyn, this is Brunhilde Meinhard."

Shakily, the older woman turned around. Her gray hair was pulled into a tight bun on top of her head. Her glasses were large with clear, plastic rims.

Jocelyn, feeling guilty for frightening the poor woman, held out her hand and gave her an apologetic smile. "Hi."

With trembling fingers and a limp, fishlike grip, Mrs. Meinhard shook Jocelyn's hand.

Suddenly uncomfortable in her skintight tank top and pajama bottoms, Jocelyn nodded politely and pointed toward her bedroom. "Well, now that I'm up, I'll go get dressed."

Neither Dr. Knight nor Mrs. Meinhard said a word. Jocelyn turned away from them.

In her bare feet, she padded down the hall, and to her chagrin, all she could think about was one thing: Her client wore pajama bottoms to bed.

Well... Thank God for that. It would have been awkward, to say the least, if he'd come flying out of his bedroom in his birthday suit. One look at him and she might have shot her gun off by mistake.

An hour later, showered and dressed, Jocelyn walked out of her room with her gun holstered under her arm, her blazer buttoned over it. She went to the kitchen to make a pot of coffee, and met Mrs. Meinhard who had already taken care of that and was now polishing the brass knobs on the white cabinetry.

"Good morning, again," Jocelyn said.

Mrs. Meinhard regarded her coolly. "Good morning."

Jocelyn poured herself a cup of coffee and watched the housekeeper scrub the hardware. "Look, I'm sorry for what happened earlier. I didn't mean to frighten you, but Dr. Knight hired me to do a job, and that's what I was doing."

Saying nothing, the woman continued to scrub.

"I guess you weren't here when the attack happened," Jocelyn continued, taking a sip of her coffee, "but is there anything you noticed that was out of place when you came in the next morning? Anything out of the ordinary that you might not have told the police?"

The woman straightened and folded her cloth. She spoke with a thick, German accent. "I tell police everything."

"I don't doubt that, ma'am. I'm just asking if there might be something you didn't think of before."

"No. There is nothing. You work for police?"

Jocelyn carefully studied the woman's face. "No, I'm a private Executive Protection Professional. E.P.P. for short."

Mrs. Meinhard nodded, but Jocelyn suspected she wasn't completely sure what that meant.

Jocelyn fired out some more questions. "Can you tell me anything about the people who visit Dr. Knight? What about friends or family? Do any of them have keys?"

She shook her head. "Doctor has no family—at least, none that come here."

"No brothers or sisters?"

"I don't know."

Jocelyn cleared her throat. How could a housekeeper, who worked in someone's home every day for four years, not know if her employer had brothers or sisters?

Then again, besides one framed picture of a young couple and a baby, there were no photographs of people anywhere, only landscapes and seascapes and old farm houses. Maybe Dr. Knight was at work most of the time when Mrs. Meinhard was here, and she was gone home when he entertained.

Still, it was strange.

"What about friends? Does his partner, Dr. Reeves, have a key? Or what about any girlfriends, past or present?"

Again, she shook her head. "No women. He goes out, but women don't' come here."

Jocelyn heard Dr. Knight's bedroom door open, and the

sound of footsteps approaching. She expected to see him in his work clothes, but instead, he wore a tank and shorts with sneakers.

He passed through the kitchen, apparently on his way to the door. "Morning."

Jocelyn set down her cup and followed him. "Wait a second, we were supposed to go over the contract this morning. Where are you going?"

"For a run." He reached the marble foyer and pulled open a small cabinet drawer to retrieve a key in a shoe wallet and fasten it to his sneaker.

"Not without me you're not," Jocelyn replied. "Did you forget what you hired me for? I'm not here to guard your penthouse. I'm here to guard *you.*"

He stared at her for a moment. "I was wondering how this was going to work…. Do you think you can keep up?"

She gave him a you've-got-to-be-kidding-me look.

"Of course you can. Sorry." He glanced down at her loafers. "Even with those?"

She glanced down, too. "Yes, with these, but I'd rather not risk an injury. Wait here and I'll change."

"You have running gear?" His voice gave away his surprise.

She flipped her hair over her shoulder as she headed to her room. "I have everything. We can discuss the contract while we run."

❧

Jocelyn placed the flat of her hands on the marble, vestibule wall, and leaned in for a calf stretch. She wore black, thigh-length Lycra shorts and a matching Y-back bra top. Her arms, shoulders and stomach were firmly toned, and just as Donovan had imagined last night as he'd watched her flicking window latches in that brown suit, she had a terrific, tight butt and long, suntanned legs to die for.

"Is there anything you *don't* do?" he asked.

She finished the stretch and bent into another one. "Cook."

"No? I love to cook."

"We'll get along well, then. You love to cook, and I love to eat what other people put in front of me."

Her delivery was deadpan, but there was something there that suggested again that she did have a sense of humor, even if she wasn't obvious about it.

Donovan suspected there was a lot more to his bodyguard than what she showed the world. No one could be as indifferent as she seemed to be, every day of their life. This had to be her professional persona, and he found himself wondering what she was like around her closest friends. He'd give anything to see her smile or laugh. Maybe he should make that his goal for the day.

Donovan continued to watch her. "Anything else you don't know how to do?"

She pulled her arm across her chest to stretch her triceps. "I don't know how to fix cars. It's on my to-do list."

"Me, neither, but I can't say it's on mine."

"No. You probably hire people to do that kind of menial work."

Donovan grabbed onto his sneaker and lifted his foot for a quad stretch. "Now, why would you say it like that? Like I'm a snob or something."

"I never said that."

"No, but you implied it with your tone, and it's not the first time."

She said nothing. She just continued to stretch.

"You're not much of a talker, are you?" Donovan asked.

"Like I said, I try to be invisible."

"Invisible is one thing. Rude is another."

"I wasn't being rude."

"Yes, you were. I asked you a question, and you ignored me."

She glanced at him briefly. "I didn't ignore you. I just didn't reply to what wasn't a question in the first place. It was an observation on your part, and you're entitled to your opinions."

Donovan stretched his hamstrings. "My opinions... God, I don't even remember what I said now. Do you always have this effect on men?"

Jocelyn ignored the last part of his question. She finished stretching and pressed the elevator button. "You said I implied you were a snob."

He snickered at her deadpan tone again, as he gazed down at her dainty profile. She was looking up at the lighted numbers over the elevator doors.

"So, did you?" he asked.

"Did I what?"

"Imply that I was a snob? You can't argue that *that* wasn't a question."

The elevator dinged, the brass doors opened and Jocelyn stepped inside. She held him back from entering, looked up at the ceiling, then motioned for him to follow. "If I implied it, I apologize. It's none of my business what kind of person you are."

Donovan pressed the lobby button. "So you don't deny it. You think I'm a snob."

Her mouth curved up in a half smile as she shook her head at him. It was a cute little smile. Slightly on the devilish side, but cute. He'd like to see another one. A looser one. The kind of smile she'd have right after sex.

If she ever had sex. He imagined there'd be a few "walls of inhibition" that would have to come down first. Or be scaled.

"What does it matter what I think, Dr. Knight? I'm just your bodyguard."

"It matters a great deal," he replied. "We're going to be in close quarters over the next little while, and call me vain, but I can't stand the idea of a woman not liking me, especially when she doesn't even know me. And why can't you call me Donovan?"

"Because our relationship is a professional one, and keeping those lines firmly drawn is important in my line of work, especially when I'm required to inhabit people's homes."

He nodded. "Ah, that makes sense. You could have said so last night, when the subject came up."

"I hadn't decided whether or not I was going to take the job last night."

The elevator reached the bottom floor, and they crossed the lobby and passed through the large revolving doors. Once out on the street, they began to jog alongside each other.

"How'd you get that scar on your left shoulder?" she asked, never taking her eyes off what was ahead of them.

"You don't miss a thing, do you? I was in a car accident a year ago."

"Your fault?"

"No, I was rammed by another driver who ran a red light. My door caved inward and broke my arm and a few ribs. The glass cut me up pretty badly, but it was all fixable. It took me a while to get back to work and back in shape. Last night you asked if I competed in triathlons. I used to, but now I'm just in training."

"You seem like an exercise nut."

"I just like keeping fit. We shouldn't take our health for granted."

They jogged a block or two, then Jocelyn said, "Let's talk about the contract now, and what level of protection you want from me."

Donovan settled into a comfortable pace, his breathing controlled. "Since you're going to be in my house anyway, we might as well go for the highest level."

"It'll cost you," she said.

"Not a problem."

They jogged down to the lights and crossed the street.

"First," she said, "let's start with your penthouse. Do you want me to arrange every improvement possible? Or stick with just the alarm system? Either way, I'll need to see your deed to ascertain if there are any conditions of occupancy that might limit what we do."

"I'll get you the deed right away, and if we can, let's go the whole nine yards. The only thing I ask is that you keep the improvements from standing out too much. I don't want my home to look like Fort Knox."

"That goes without saying. I already put together some ideas last night with that in mind, since I figured cosmetics would be important to you."

Donovan swerved around a spilled ice-cream cone on the sidewalk. "There you go again."

"What do you mean, 'there I go again'?" Her voice got a little haughty, and Donovan couldn't deny that he liked it. She was inching off that rock of indifference.

"The way you figured cosmetics would be important to me. Now you're implying that I'm shallow."

She laughed out loud, and it was everything he had hoped it would be—throaty and from the heart. "I implied no such thing!"

They crossed the street and headed toward Lincoln Park, their running shoes tapping the ground in perfect unison. Donovan had to admit he enjoyed needling her, to open her up a little, and he wasn't sure why. He never felt the urge to prod the women he usually dated and get to know more about what they were like deep down. It was usually the other way around.

She was quiet for a moment. "Can we get back to the contract now?"

They jogged onto the running track in the park, and passed other runners along the way. "Sure. You were talking about the penthouse."

"Yes. I'll act as your contractor, hiring the appropriate experts to install a new alarm system and make your doors and windows more secure. As far as personal protection, I'll accompany you everywhere for a daily fee, which will be payable every thirty days."

"Even to work?"

"You said you wanted the highest level of protection."

"I do, but I'm a heart surgeon. You'll have to sit in the waiting room a lot. You won't find that tiresome?"

"It's my job, to do whatever's necessary."

"What about days off? Surely you'll need holidays."

"I take holidays between jobs," she said.

"What if you get sick?"

"I have colleagues I trust with my life, and we spell each other off in emergencies like that."

Donovan felt sweat cooling his back between his shoulder blades. Jocelyn had a healthy glow on her face, too, but she wasn't working too hard, not by a long shot. She was clearly in great shape.

"I thought you worked alone," he said.

"I do, but I didn't always."

He considered that. "These colleagues…buddies from the Secret Service?"

"That's right. There are a number of us who work privately now. We contract each other out whenever we require team details."

They jogged in silence along the water, in perfect sync with each other, enjoying the fresh, early morning air. For a long time neither of them said anything, until they came to the end of the park.

"Ready to turn back?" Jocelyn asked.

"Yeah, I usually go that way." He pointed.

She stopped and bent forward, her hands on her knees as she tried to talk through deep breaths. "Really? We should go a different way then, and run elsewhere tomorrow."

He understood what she was getting at—it was a security thing—and nodded in the other direction. "That way through the park will take a little longer, but we'll end up back where we started."

"Great." They began to run again, both of them covered in a shiny film of perspiration, but still keeping perfect pace. When they arrived back on Donovan's street, they walked for a bit to cool down before going inside. They passed by the security guard, who politely waved.

Jocelyn got on the elevator first, and like before, checked the ceiling before letting him get on.

"What are you looking for?" he asked, as he stepped inside.

"If the hatch is ajar, there could be someone up there."

"Do you really think that's likely?"

She shrugged. "Can't take any chances."

On the way up to his penthouse, Donovan was intensely aware of the silence between them, and had to stop himself from gazing down at her just for the sheer pleasure of it.

God, she smelled good. Like the outdoors and fresh, clean sweat. His blood began to pulse in his veins, and for the first time in years, he felt nervous around a woman.

"Maybe on the way to your office this morning," she said, "we could talk about suspects."

He tried to imagine that. "We could, if you don't mind people listening in."

"What do you mean? What people?"

"The people on the El."

The doors opened, and he stepped off, but Jocelyn stayed on the elevator. Donovan had to put his arm in front of the door to keep it from closing while she was still inside.

"You take the *train* to your office?" she asked, sounding more than a little surprised.

Donovan couldn't help but smile, and this time, she smiled back.

"I'm doing it again, aren't I?" she asked.

"Yes, you are. I suppose you expected me to have a limo and driver?"

At last she stepped off the elevator and held her

hands up in mock surrender. "Guilty as charged. No more assumptions, I promise."

Donovan paused in the vestibule. "Why do you have those impressions of me, anyway? Is it because I was wearing a tux last night? Do you think my life is one big cocktail party?"

She shrugged. "Something like that. You have to admit, though, appearances haven't exactly made you out to be Blue Collar Joe."

Laughing quietly, Donovan bent down to get his key out of his shoe wallet, then straightened. "I'm a pretty normal guy, you know."

"Sure. A normal guy who has the best of everything in one of the most expensive penthouses in downtown Chicago."

"You're very observant, I'll give you that, but what you see is not always all that's there. You can't possibly know what's going on *inside* a person, by seeing what kind of beer they drink or what kind of house they live in."

She rubbed her perspiring forehead. "Appearances speak volumes about a person. Already I know that you like things to be perfect in your physical life, and you lack depth in the relationships in your personal life."

Donovan felt his hackles rise. "Lack depth? God, it's one insult after another! Why would you think that about me?"

"Because I see how perfect everything is in your penthouse, and clearly with all the exercise and working out you do, the perfection of your physical appearance is very important to you. You don't have any close friends or family who visit you, and you have voicemails from seven women, all waiting to be called back."

He brow furrowed. "You listened to my messages?"

"You said I could go through your underwear drawer if I wanted. I didn't think your messages were too far a stretch, and I was looking for clues about possible stalkers."

"And you think you found them."

She shrugged again. "Disgruntled ex-lovers are classic suspects."

Donovan inserted the key into the lock but didn't open the door. There was a lot he could tell her about his personal life to correct her on her superficial impressions of him, but the last thing he wanted to do right now, while he was boiling mad, was become defensive and pour his soul out on the floor at her feet. Instead, he turned the tables on her.

"You think you've got me figured out, but what I want to know is, who are *you* to judge *me,* when you are clearly hiding inside a tough, cold exterior that shouts at the world to keep out? Answer that, Ms. Mackenzie, and I promise I won't ask you any more personal questions for the duration of our professional relationship."

He took some pleasure from the fact that he'd obviously knocked her composure off-kilter. Her full lips were parted in astonishment, as if she had no idea what to say.

Then he added with a bite, "That is, *if* this relationship lasts beyond a day. Cuz I sure as hell didn't intend to hire a bodyguard who thinks she's a psychologist."

H *iding behind a tough, cold exterior that shouts at the world to keep out?* Was that how he saw her?

For a few uncomfortable seconds, Jocelyn reflected upon Dr. Knight's passionate assessment of her. *Good Lord,* when had she turned into such a cold fish? Had she been alone too long and forgotten how to connect with people? Or was she dispassionate because she'd been dragged through the dirt by most of the people she'd allowed herself to trust?

Her heart stung suddenly with a memory of being about five years old, climbing onto her father's lap for a hug, and being shoved off and yelled at because her fingers were sticky.

Was that why she'd stopped trying to be close to people? Because of all the moments like those in her childhood?

Jocelyn gazed up at Donovan, then consciously swept away any concerns about her personality or demeanor, for it was not in her nature to feel sorry for herself, nor was this the time to be reflecting on her less than perfect childhood.

And hey, it was her job to be tough, and personally detached.

She would have liked to tell him that, but she decided it would be completely unprofessional to enter into a debate with a client about the workings of her inner self. Best to just back down.

"I'm guilty again," Jocelyn said, as they stood outside his door. "I judged you. I admit it. You're right, I don't know you very well and I'm sorry. Obviously there's more to you than I thought."

A great deal more, or you wouldn't be so interested in what's going on with me, her inner voice added.

"Now you're just trying to please your client."

"I'm sorry, all right?"

He looked taken aback. "You give in awfully easy for a tough as nails bodyguard."

Jocelyn huffed. "It's my job to *prevent* showdowns, not engage the enemy unless absolutely necessary."

"And now you're calling me the enemy."

She shook her head and almost laughed. "No, I'm not."

"Well, I'm glad we got that clear."

They stood in the vestibule for a moment, staring at each other.

He blinked slowly at her. "You should give in more often, you know."

A sudden image of giving in to him in other ways burned in her brain, but she didn't want to go down *that* road. "I beg your pardon?"

"Your face…" He reached up to touch the center of her forehead with his thumb. "All the tension right here. It's gone. You look…softer."

His thumb feathered along her eyebrow before he lowered his hand to his side, and she didn't know what to say. The line had been crossed, and she wasn't used to being on this side of it—suddenly weak-kneed and foggy-brained with a client, after an inappropriate conversation about her character, a conversation that had left her contemplating her childhood.

She wet her lips and fought to keep her breathing steady.

"You can relax," he said, "I'm still going to hire you."

"I'm perfectly relaxed."

"Yeah? I don't think so." He chuckled, which told her that he was arrogantly aware of his ability to reduce women to simpering blobs of jelly whenever he felt the urge.

But Jocelyn wasn't like most women. She knew how to steel herself against such responses. "I'm not one of your girlfriends, you know. And trust me, you don't want me to be *soft*."

He nodded. "You're probably right, under the circumstances."

He unlocked and pushed open the door to his penthouse, but Jocelyn wrapped her hand around his muscular, sweaty upper arm to stop him from going in first.

"Mrs. Meinhard?" she asked, crossing the threshold ahead of him. "Are you here?"

"In the kitchen!" the woman called out.

"Is everything as it should be?"

"It's fine, thank you!"

Nevertheless, Jocelyn had Donovan wait inside by the door while she quickly checked out the penthouse.

That night, after returning home from a long day in the hospital, Donovan changed into a pair of faded blue jeans and T-shirt, then sank onto his plush, white sofa. He had just ordered Chinese food, and Jocelyn had gone into her room for a few minutes to make sure the alarm system would be installed tomorrow as scheduled.

He stared at the dark windows, enjoying the silence for a moment, thinking about their conversation in the vestibule that morning.

When he'd gone up against all her judgmental observations with one of his own, he had completely disarmed her. She'd backed down quicker than a spooked rabbit.

What was her story? She didn't want him getting into her personal life, yet she was perfectly comfortable and eager to probe into his.

She would probably argue that it was the nature of her job—to learn everything she could about the people she was sworn to protect—but he didn't buy that. When he'd commented on *her* personal life, he'd knocked her completely off balance.

Why also, he wondered, did she have such strong negative opinions about his lifestyle? He wasn't a criminal, yet she looked upon him—and everything he owned—with disapproval.

He stood up, went to his iPod which was docked in the speaker system, and set it to play *Eric Clapton, Unplugged,* to try and clear his head. Sounds of a jazzy guitar filled the room, and within seconds, Jocelyn came down the hall, still wearing her brown trousers and buttoned-up white blouse, although her blouse was slightly untucked on one side.

She paused and listened to the music. "Eric Clapton."

"Yeah."

Jocelyn stood in the arched entry to the living room with her hand on one of the white columns, then moved more fully into the room. "I haven't heard this in ages. I used to listen to it in my car. I drove to Florida once for a vacation, and played it over and over."

He nodded as she sat down on one end of the sofa. "When was that?"

"Oh…four years ago. I think that's the last time I took a real vacation."

"Sounds like it might be time for another."

"Not really. I like working."

He sat down at the opposite end of the sofa. "Everybody needs time off."

"I get time off between assignments, although I'm usually doing the advance work for the next one. But you know what they say—a change is as good as a rest."

"Maybe." Just then, the doorbell chimed. "It's the food." Donovan stood to answer it, but Jocelyn stopped him.

"Let me." She went to the door and used the peephole, then opened it using the chain. "How much, please?"

The delivery man told her. "Just a minute." She closed the door again and locked it.

Donovan was right behind her with a couple of bills. "He can keep the change."

She opened the door and paid the man, then closed it and turned all the locks again.

"You certainly are thorough," he said, carrying the large paper bag toward the kitchen.

"That's what you're paying me for."

She followed him into the kitchen. They pulled the white boxes out of the bag and set them on the large, marble-topped center island. Jocelyn pulled out the wooden chopsticks.

"I have better ones here somewhere," Donovan said, opening drawers until he found his good set. He fetched plates, then sat next to Jocelyn on one of the stools.

They popped open a couple of cans of ginger ale, then served themselves and began to eat.

"You have a beautiful formal dining room, and I suppose you eat here most of the time."

"Yeah, I do. Everything's handy here, and it's just usually me anyway."

"But I thought you liked to cook." She poured her fizzing ginger ale into a glass. "I'd imagined you inviting dinner companions over, to impress them with your gourmet meals and fancy cutlery."

He drew his eyebrows together to give her a look that told her she was doing it again.

She covered her mouth with a hand. "Sorry."

"Apology accepted, on one condition."

"I don't like the sound of that." Her playful tone sparked a pleasant awareness of her as a woman.

"Don't worry," he replied. "It's nothing indecent. Not that I wouldn't enjoy a little indecency with you, but I doubt it's in your job description."

She gave him a warning look. "That is totally inappropriate, Donovan."

Hearing her use his given name for the first time sent his pulse on a bumpy road trip, but at the same time, he felt like a heel for having made that comment.

"I apologize again," he said soberly. "I'm just not used to having a beautiful woman in my house twenty-four hours a day."

She wiped her mouth with a napkin. "Let's get this straight. I'm not a beautiful woman. I'm your bodyguard. And what would you be talking about if I were a man?"

"Football, probably."

She swallowed another bite. "Well, I don't want to talk about football, but we're both adults and you need to remember why I'm here. Someone might be trying to kill you, and I can't afford to lose my focus. So no hanky panky, please."

He nodded, feeling very much put in his place, which was only right.

Jocelyn sipped her ginger ale. "You still haven't told me the condition involved in your accepting my apology."

"Ah, yes. The condition." He wiped his mouth with a napkin. "Well, you've expressed these somewhat biased perceptions of me more than once, and I'd like to know why you have them, or more importantly, why you seem to disapprove of me."

She inhaled deeply and moved her spring roll around on her plate with a chopstick. "I don't disapprove of you. I barely know you."

"You *do* disapprove of me, and you're also great at avoiding questions."

"And you're great at being bold."

"Still avoiding."

She chuckled softly, then gazed at him, incredulously. "You don't give up, do you?"

"Nope."

Eric Clapton's "Layla" started to play in the other room, its mellow rhythm easing the tension-filled silence. Donovan watched Jocelyn lean against the wrought iron back of the bar stool. Her lips were glossy from the cherry sauce.

His body began to react to the image of his mouth on hers, so he swerved his thoughts back around to what he and Jocelyn had been talking about a few seconds ago. He'd asked her a question and she hadn't answered it yet.

He waited.

And waited.

She poked at her stir-fried veggies. "All right, if you must know, I used to be involved with a doctor, years ago. Only he wasn't a doctor at the time. He was in medical school."

Donovan considered that. "What, the guy was a jerk, so all doctors are jerks? Or you're not over him, and I remind you of it?"

"No, it's neither of those things," she replied.

"What is it then?"

Lord, talking to her was like getting blood from a stone.

She took a sip of her ginger ale. "We lived together when he was going through school, and I supported both of us while I put off going to the police academy. Then, as soon as he graduated, he dumped me and went off to marry some rich debutante, and basically changed his whole identity. He bought a Mercedes Benz, started going to the opera and ballet, when he was never into that sort of thing with me. We used to go to hockey games and sports pubs where the draft was cheap. I guess the worst part was that he'd been seeing this woman while he was still with me. He lied to me and left me with all the debt I'd incurred to support us while he was in school, and never looked back. I met him once a couple of years ago in a bookstore, and he was with his wife. He never spoke to me or introduced me to her. They both looked at me like I was dirt under their shoes—in another class far below them."

"So that's why you disapprove of me? You think that just because I own a penthouse and go to the opera occasionally, I'm a stuffed shirt?"

He hoped she realized how mistaken she was. He hadn't grown up with this wealth. He had come into it later when he would have given anything to trade it for what he'd lost. He'd trade every last cent of it today and live like a pauper, if it meant he could change his childhood, and see and touch the parents he never really knew. Even just for a second.

He tried to summon a memory or two—his mother's loving smile, his father's boisterous laughter, but there were only fragments of what seemed like a dream. If only he could remember more…

"It's not just that," Jocelyn replied, and gestured around the room with her hand. "Tom became a doctor to have all of this. For the prestige. The material wealth. It had nothing to do with wanting to help people. This kind of lifestyle was more important to him than any patient ever could be."

Donovan sat back. "I see, and because I'm a successful doctor and live alone in a penthouse, and I have women leaving messages on my answering machine, I don't care about people, either?"

She shrugged.

"You really don't know much about me, Jocelyn. You realize that, don't you?"

Nodding, she seemed to agree. He was glad. Maybe he'd give her the whole story sometime.

Donovan gazed at her face while she fiddled with her food. She'd barely eaten half of what was on her plate.

"Look," he said, "I didn't mean to put you on the spot or make you feel bad or anything."

"I don't feel bad."

He lightened his tone, smiling. "Yes, you do."

Thank goodness she smiled, too. She picked up her fortune cookie, wrapped in plastic, and hurled it across the corner of the island to hit him in the chest. "I don't."

Donovan laughed. "Okay, okay."

He picked up the cookie. "Is this yours or mine? I don't want to mess with fate and get the wrong fortune."

She picked up the other one. "It's yours. I'll take this one."

They both opened their packets. "What does yours say?" he asked.

"It says, 'You are a deep, complex individual.' What about yours?"

"Hmm. Let me see." He broke the cookie and unfurled the little piece of paper. "Wow. It says, 'You're going to get lucky tonight.' What do you think it means by that?"

Her lips parted. "Let me see that!" She grabbed it out of his hands. "It does *not* say that, you big jerk. It says 'You like to fix things.'"

She handed it back to him, then she rose to clean away the dishes and put the leftovers in the fridge. "Nice try though."

Donovan watched her from behind. Unfortunately, not nice enough.

He was a brilliant cardiovascular surgeon, Jocelyn had learned from just about everyone she talked to about Donovan at the hospital. The best around. Nice man, too, they all said, including the nurses, who didn't seem to imply that he ever tried to make moves on them, which was somewhat surprising to Jocelyn, considering some of the flirty conversations they'd had since she took this job.

He'd made no secret of the fact that he thought she was hot stuff, but he never truly crossed the line and he'd behaved himself perfectly since those first twenty-four hours. She couldn't deny it had been flattering, especially because she'd never imagined herself as "hot." She wore plain suits and flat shoes to work, sensible cotton underwear. She always wore her hair in a ponytail and she was definitely *not* a flirt. In fact, she made a conscious effort not to give off those signals—at least the kind that alerted hungry male hormones to a potential meal. Consequently, she considered herself rather dull.

In her defense, being dull came with the job. She didn't

go places with her principals to be a part of their social lives. She wanted to blend in, to be polite and generally not speak unless spoken to, and where possible be invisible. In addition to that, she had to be paranoid all the time and maintain an attitude that no one was to be trusted, which didn't exactly make her Miss Congeniality at social functions.

Jocelyn lowered her magazine, feeling suddenly dissatisfied. All her life, she'd always made a conscious effort to be invisible, even outside of work, whether it was in the way she dressed or the way she talked.

Why? Because when she was a kid, she'd been taught to act cute in front of the neighbors and wear fancy dresses with lace, her hair in shiny curls? Was it because *that* was the only time her parents praised her—when her appearance was perfect—and this was some sort of rebellion against that kind of shallow thinking?

She continued to flip through the fashion magazine, looking at all the skinny, glamorous models with big hair and small boobs. *Blah*. She felt sorry for them, and she certainly didn't want to compare herself to them. It was what was on the inside that mattered.

She shut the magazine and tossed it onto the table in front of her chair.

The door to Donovan's office opened just then, and a middle-aged woman walked out. Donovan, wearing a cotton shirt and jeans and sneakers beneath his lab coat, followed her out. She stopped at the reception desk to speak to the nurse, and was laughing at something Donovan was saying to her.

Carrying his clipboard, he turned away from her and said, "Enjoy yourself at the golf tournament, Marion."

He was certainly charming, and appeared very caring with his patients. He seemed less and less like Tom every day. No wonder everyone liked him.

He passed through the waiting room and glanced down at Jocelyn, who sat in a chair among the other patients.

"Bored yet?" he softly asked, so no one else could hear.

"Not at all." She smiled dutifully and opened up another magazine, while Donovan invited the next patient in—an elderly gentleman with a walker.

"George, how are we doing today?" Donovan asked the man, just before he closed the door behind him.

Jocelyn continued to flip idly through her magazine, repeating to herself over and over in her head: *He's your client. That's all. Your client, your client, your client.*

⁓ℰ

Contrary to Donovan's normal routine of taking the train to work and back, they started taking his car, as Jocelyn didn't feel it was safe to walk to the train at the same time each morning, or stand in the crowded compartment, where anyone could pull a knife without warning and be gone just as fast.

In the parking lot after work, she conducted her usual vehicle search before allowing Donovan to get in. She began by checking the small pieces of tape she routinely affixed at inconspicuous spots along the door, hood and trunk openings, to detect if the vehicle had been tampered with during the day. Then she proceeded with a detailed search of the interior and exterior of the car, looking for trip wires, stripped screws, leaking fluids and such. Donovan waited nearby, watching.

She gave the vehicle a clean bill of health and got in. Donovan got behind the wheel and they headed home.

"How about dinner and the theater tonight?" he asked her, shifting gears and gaining speed out on the main road.

The question caught her off guard. Principals didn't usually ask her to dinner with them—not phrased like that anyway.

He gave her a perceptive, sidelong glance, taking his eyes off the road only momentarily. "What I should have said is: 'I'm going to eat out tonight and take in a play. I'll need you to work late.'"

Jocelyn smiled, appreciating his courteous rephrasing of the invitation. "Yes, sir."

"And I'd like to go to an upscale place for dinner, and I don't want to be conspicuous with you standing over my shoulder or hovering around the back of the room, so if you're going to fit in, you won't be able to wear that. And I'd prefer that you sit at the table and eat with me."

She glanced down at her suit. "I don't really have anything with me that's—"

"We'll get you something on the way home." He turned down a street in the opposite direction from where he lived.

"Really, you don't have to buy me clothes," Jocelyn said. "We can stop by my apartment and I can pick something up."

"You live on the other side of town. This'll be quicker. I know a great spot."

She reluctantly agreed, and they drove down a narrow, tree-lined street. Donovan pulled up in front of an exclusive ladies' boutique on the bottom floor of a late-Victorian mansion, and turned off the car. "What are you…a size two?"

"Five, actually," she replied awkwardly.

"Great. Let's go."

He led the way in, and bells chimed over the door as they entered. An older lady with her hair in a bun, wearing a pale yellow silk suit and pearls, approached. "Dr. Knight, what a pleasure. What can I help you with today?"

They know him here?

"Actually, Doris, you can help my friend. We're going to La Perla tonight."

"Lovely." She turned her warm gaze toward Jocelyn, who felt painfully out of place in this high-end clothing shop.

"I have some wonderful little numbers over here that would look stunning on you," Doris said. She gestured for Jocelyn to follow. Donovan followed, too. Doris picked a navy sequined dress off a brass rack. "What about this?"

Jocelyn glanced down at the tag. The dress cost nine hundred and fifty dollars. "Um, that might be a little too…"

"Too flashy?" Doris said. "I understand. What about this one?" The smiling woman moved to another rack and presented a deep crimson off-the-shoulder dress. It was twelve hundred dollars.

Jocelyn touched her index finger to her lips. "That, I think, is…um…"

"Not the right color?"

Not the right price! "Yes, exactly."

"Okay, I think I know exactly what you're looking for." Doris moved to the corner of the boutique and found a short-sleeved black, curve-hugging dress with a few clear gemstones at the collar. "Perfect for La Perla."

"Perfect for Jocelyn," Donovan said, moving past her and touching the delicate fabric.

Jocelyn didn't dare look at the price tag on that one. The odd thing was, Donovan didn't look at it, either.

She shook her head in utter disbelief. *The rich.* Feeling more than a little uncomfortable with all this, Jocelyn looped her arm through Donovan's and gently pulled him away from Doris. "Could I have a word with you?" she whispered politely.

"Sure." They moved behind a mannequin dressed in a sailing outfit.

"This is too much," Jocelyn whispered. "I can't let you buy me a dress here."

"Why not?" he asked innocently.

"Because it's too expensive. I couldn't possibly accept a gift like this."

"It's not *that* expensive. Not relatively."

"Relative to what?"

He paused. "I don't know... To other shops. Really, twelve hundred's not that much for a dress like that."

"What, twelve *thousand* would be more in line with what you'd call expensive?"

"Well, yeah."

She felt the difference between them like a deep chasm at that moment. Twelve hundred dollars was pocket change to him.

"And how do you know about prices of dresses anyway?" she asked, still whispering. "And how does Doris know your name? Do you come here all the time to buy clothes for your lady friends? The ones who leave messages on your answering machine? The ones you never call back?"

He raised his eyebrows, looking amused. "You sound jealous."

"I am *not* jealous. I just find it odd that the clerk here knows you by name and—and I'm not one of those women. I'm your bodyguard."

"What about this one?" Doris said, appearing unexpectedly behind Jocelyn, who felt her face color.

"I liked the other one better," Donovan said.

Doris went away, and he took a step closer to Jocelyn to whisper in her ear. "Why don't you just try it on? I really want to go out to dinner tonight, and like I said before, you can't wear that."

His hot breath in her ear sent goose bumps down the left side of her body, and she had to work hard to ignore them.

"Why not?" she asked. "This isn't a date. I'm just there for your security. You don't need to dress me up like a princess. That's not who I am."

"You said yourself that you prefer to blend in, not be conspicuous. This is appropriate for where we're going."

Jocelyn gazed at his imploring expression, then remembered one of the strict rules of her profession: The words "It's not my job" should never be uttered.

It was her duty to always ensure that her principal felt secure and comfortable, whether that meant raising an umbrella over his head if it started to rain, or making sure that his luggage didn't get lost on a flight across the country. In this case, if seeing her dressed to "fit in" with the clientele at the restaurant would make him feel more at ease, then she had to do as she was asked.

With a sigh of defeat, she raised her hands in the air. "All right, I'll try it on."

"Thank you," he whispered close to her ear, causing another wave of goose bumps across her skin.

Doris led her into an enormous wallpapered change room with a small mahogany table and lamp inside, as well as an upholstered settee. There were three pairs of patent leather shoes on a low shelf, for the customers to use.

Man oh man, this was *so* not her life.

She tried on the dress, slipped the heels on her feet, then turned to look at herself in the mirror.

Her heart almost skipped a beat. It had to be someone else's reflection she was looking at. The dress hugged all her curves—curves she wasn't even aware she possessed—and made her look sophisticated and radiant, like a movie star on the red carpet. *Like a woman.*

A knock sounded at the dressing room door. "How are you doing in there?" Doris asked. "Can I get you anything?"

Feeling uncertain and turning around carefully—for she wasn't used to walking in heels—Jocelyn slowly grasped the crystal knob and stepped out. She tried to ignore how uncomfortable and ridiculous she felt.

Doris smiled and nodded. "That's the one."

Jocelyn, who had kept her head down since she'd opened the door, finally looked up. Donovan's gaze was moving slowly up and down the length of her body.

Her heart held still, waiting for what he might say, while she chided herself for letting it matter. She shouldn't care what she looked like in his eyes. In fact, she should hate the fact that he wanted to dress her up like this. She wasn't a doll or an ornament.

Yet, another part of her felt oddly liberated seeing herself this way. All through her life she had resisted any desire to wear something pretty, to feel soft and feminine, because she didn't want to be valued for that. She wanted to be valued for her character and her mind.

Contemplatively, Donovan tilted his head to the side and smiled. "Yes, this is definitely the one."

~⊘

The restaurant was small, intimate and very romantic.

Located in the low-ceilinged basement of an old stone mansion in a quiet part of town, it was dimly lit with flickering candles and staffed with soft-spoken waiters in tuxedos. White-clothed tables—set with sparkling crystal wineglasses and shiny silver utensils—were spaced apart in little alcoves or surrounded by creeping ivy plants to provide privacy. It was the perfect place for a discreet affair.

Jocelyn had called ahead to arrange for cooperation regarding Donovan's security, and had ascertained that this would be a low-risk detail, judging by the floor plan the manager had faxed over to her. Still, she kept her gun strapped to her ankle and looked around the restaurant with discerning eyes as they were led to their table in the back corner.

"So this is where the theater crowd comes?" Jocelyn commented, sitting down while Donovan stood behind her and slid her chair forward.

He took the seat across from her. Behind him, a trellis of greenery closed him in. The gray stone wall provided enclosure. The waiter poured water for them and Donovan ordered wine.

"So you never told me how you know Doris," Jocelyn said, making conversation after the waiter disappeared.

Donovan's lips curved up in a slow-burning smile. "Have you been carrying that question around all afternoon and evening?"

"Really, I haven't given it a thought until now."

He gave her an exaggerated, knowing nod that told her he was completely aware that she had been curious since they'd left the shop, and he was amused by it.

"If you must know, Doris was a patient of mine," he said.

Oh.

Jocelyn continued to gaze at him, realizing she'd jumped to conclusions again, and deciding that tonight, she was going to, at long last, figure this man out, and prove or disprove every first and last mistaken impression she had of him.

"I can't tell you more than that," he continued, "because of doctor-patient confidentiality, only that I trust her good taste."

"I see. I thought…"

He was amused again. The playful tone in his voice revealed it. "I know what you thought—that I take all my lovers there to dress them up to my liking, or impress them and buy favors."

Jocelyn shook her head at herself and grinned apologetically. This was ridiculous. She had to get her act together.

"Donovan," she said point-blank. "If we're going to have any kind of normal working relationship, it's time I did some intelligence gathering."

"Intelligence gathering? Jocelyn, you're a riot. How about we just have a conversation, like two normal people out to dinner together, getting to know each other?"

She nervously cleared her throat. Where were her social skills when she needed them? She supposed—on top of her glamorous attire this evening—she wasn't used to clients taking her out to quiet, romantic restaurants for dinner. Usually, she, in her flat brown shoes and starchy white shirt, sat at a nearby table alone while her clients had dinner with *other* people.

But apparently, Donovan wanted this to be like a date, and she had no idea how to behave with a rich, handsome surgeon who knew which fork to use and how to order the best wine to go along with the meal.

Add to that the complexity of her trying to behave professionally and *not* be charming—as if she would know how—for she didn't want this to be too enjoyable for either one of them. That could lead to dangerous places.

"All right," she said nonetheless. "Let's get to know each other. How about we start with the voicemails on your home phone? How is it possible that you could be seeing seven women at the same time? Do they know about each other?"

She made sure to keep her tone light and friendly, so she wouldn't come off sounding like she was jealous.

Donovan leaned back in his chair. "I'm not actually *seeing* any of them. We're all mostly just friends."

"Mostly."

He wet his lips. "I'm thirty-four years old, Jocelyn. I'm not a monk."

If this wasn't such a high-class joint, and she wasn't wearing these ridiculous strappy heels, she would have crawled under the table and cringed, and stayed there until after dessert was served. "Of course, I didn't mean to imply…"

"It's okay. That's what we're doing tonight, isn't it? Cutting to the chase? While we're on the topic of those women, I might as well tell you that I'm not involved with any of them now. I've been busy lately and keeping to myself. I haven't had much of a social life, and contrary to what you might think, those messages you heard didn't all come the day you arrived. They've been accumulating over the past couple of months, and I've been saving them only because I never seem to get around to returning the calls."

"But what if they've all been sitting by the phone all this time, waiting for you to call?"

"I doubt any of them have been sitting by their phones, at least not over me. They'd move on to the next guy pretty quickly."

"How can you be so sure? Maybe one or two of them truly are waiting for you to call. Maybe you're treating them carelessly and you don't realize it."

"No, Jocelyn, I wouldn't do that." His voice was so direct, his tone so indisputable, she couldn't even contemplate not believing him. "Besides, none of them ever had their hearts invested in me. It was only their ambitions."

"Their ambitions?"

"Yes. You know, the Won't-Mother-be-proud-if-I-snag-myself-a-rich-doctor kind of ambitions."

"How do you know?"

"I *just know*. And I never wanted that kind of a superficial relationship, no matter how attractive or successful a woman was."

Jocelyn gazed into his appealing green eyes, and felt stunned by everything he was saying. She knew she had been misjudging him all this time, but she'd had no idea to what extreme. She'd imagined he was the kind of man who would use other people for his own enjoyment, but in fact, it seemed to be the other way around. He was the one being used, and he—as far as she could tell—didn't like it.

Shallow, he was not.

"Is that why you've never married?"

"Yes and no. I haven't met the right woman, certainly, but I haven't really been looking, either. Marriage just isn't at the top of my to-do list these days."

"So what's been keeping you so busy lately?" she asked, changing the subject. "Besides watching out for stalkers?"

"I've been raising funds for a grief counseling center for children."

Her head drew back in surprise. "No kidding."

The waiter brought the wine and Donovan tasted it and gave it the proverbial thumbs-up. The waiter began to pour some in Jocelyn's glass, but she stopped him after the first splash.

"That's enough, thank you." She never drank on the job.

"Are you ever going to let your hair down around me?" Donovan asked, when the waiter left them alone.

"My hair *is* down."

"And it looks beautiful by the way. But you know what I mean. Are you ever going to forget that you're my bodyguard, and just be a woman? Even for a couple of hours when the threats against my person are minimal?"

Jocelyn cleared her throat. The implications of that question were disturbing to say the least, especially the way she'd been feeling lately.

"That might be dangerous. If I let down my guard, even for a minute, that would be the time something disastrous would happen. Rule of the trade."

That wasn't the only reason why it would be disastrous, but she didn't want to go there.

Donovan sat across from Jocelyn, admiring the way she

looked in the flickering candlelight, wearing that elegant off-the-shoulder black dress with the earrings Doris had helped her pick out to match.

He could tell by the way Jocelyn carried herself that she had absolutely no idea—not a clue—how incredibly beautiful she was.

Or how she was driving him insane keeping him on this side of the table, with the bodyguard-principal lines so firmly drawn. He'd chosen this restaurant for a reason, so she could relax for a few hours between walking in and walking out, and he could have a chance to try and bring out the woman in her.

Because he knew there was a real woman in there—a fascinating and passionate one—buried somewhere deep down inside, and anxious to come out. He could see it in her mysterious, dazzling eyes.

He wasn't imagining that there was something between them, either—something she was fighting with all her might.

The waiter returned and took their orders, then made a slight bow and departed.

"So why have *you* never married?" Donovan asked before taking a long sip of wine. He noticed she didn't touch hers.

She leaned forward, put her elbow on the table and rested her chin on her hand. "I don't really believe in happily ever after, and I prefer being on my own."

"Do you really?"

"Yes, I do."

"What about your parents? Where are they?"

"My mother died six years ago, and my father is somewhere in the Midwest."

"You don't know where he lives?"

"No, my parents divorced when I was fourteen, and he never kept in touch. It was best that way. It would have been too hard on my mother to see him. He broke her heart when he left her for a younger woman. I guess he wanted a trophy wife."

Donovan reached across the table and touched her hand. "I'm sorry to hear that. She never remarried?"

"No, and I can't blame her. After what Dad did, it would've been pretty hard to trust anyone again."

His tough-as-nails, untouchable bodyguard was becoming more clear to Donovan by the minute. The only two men she'd ever been close to had both left her for something shinier and never looked back. She was bound to be wary of relationships.

A few minutes later, their appetizers arrived, and they talked about other things. Jocelyn told him about her experiences in the Secret Service, as well as what it was like going through the police academy. Some of her stories were downright hilarious, and she had him in stitches with a few of her tales. There were some hair-raising incidents, too, when she had come face-to-face with attackers on the wife of a former vice-president, and had to use her combat skills. Mostly, though, she described her job as being pretty quiet. Prevention was everything.

After dinner, they drove to the theater where they sat in Donovan's regular box seats, and Jocelyn seemed to enjoy the play immensely. When they finally arrived home it was almost midnight, and they rode up in the elevator, smiling and talking about the actors.

When they reached the top floor, Jocelyn removed her heels in the vestibule, opened the door and disarmed the new, state-of-the-art alarm system inside, then searched the penthouse thoroughly. Once she'd ensured everything was fine, she returned to where Donovan waited near the door.

"Everything's clear. We can relax now."

"We can?" He tried not to think of all the ways he would like to relax with this incredible woman he had invited into his home. This beautiful, appealing, sexy woman who set his blood on fire.

"Since you put it like that, how about joining me for a nightcap?"

"You know I don't drink on the—"

"On the job, yeah I know, but we're home now and you've already searched the place. The new alarm system is up and running for later in the night. Surely you can consider yourself off duty for the next hour. Just one glass of wine. Or pop. Your choice."

Jocelyn sighed heavily. "I haven't had a glass of wine in eons."

He spread his hands wide. "I have just about every kind you can imagine—Shiraz, merlot, sauvignon blanc, Chardonnay—you name it."

"Well, I did want to talk to you some more about who could be stalking you."

"We can talk about whatever you want."

She hesitated for a few seconds. "I guess one glass of Shiraz wouldn't hurt."

"Excellent." He backed away from her toward the kitchen. "Don't go away. I'll bring it to you. Just make yourself comfortable."

Donovan left Jocelyn in the living room and went to pour two glasses of the best red wine he had in his collection.

Donovan brought the wine into the living room where Jocelyn sat, curled up on his huge white sofa.

He stopped in the entranceway. *God help him*, he couldn't get over how incredible she looked in that slinky, black dress. It set off the ebony color of her hair and complemented the creamy whiteness of her complexion. It brought out her full, rose-petal lips. She didn't look like a bodyguard. She looked like a goddess.

"This really is a beautiful home you have, Donovan," she said, looking up at him. "I haven't said it before, but it's very inviting. And this sofa—I could get lost in it."

She stroked the soft upholstery with a graceful hand.

Donovan stood motionless, watching her long slender arm move back and forth across the cushions.

His blood quickened in his veins. What he wouldn't give to be one of those cushions now....

Groping for his equilibrium, he fully entered the room and handed a glass to her, then sat down on the sofa.

"I had a great time tonight," he said. "We should do it again."

She looked at him with those big brown eyes over the rim of her glass as she took the first sip, then set her glass on the coffee table. "I had a nice time, too, but I'm not so sure we should do it again."

"And why is that?"

But he suspected he knew why. *Here it comes....*

"Because I wouldn't want us to have *too* good a time together," she explained.

He exhaled heavily. "I see. Because that might lead to something we'd both enjoy, and we can't have that. You have a job to do. Better that we don't get to know each other at all. Right?"

She peered down at her glass. "We don't have to ignore each other completely. But you know what I mean. Our relationship is a professional one, and you're paying me a lot of money. I don't want any lines to get blurred about what 'services' I'm expected to provide here."

He gazed at her feminine profile, feeling the pulse of his heart, the hum of his blood through his body. "You know I would never take advantage of you like that, Jocelyn. That's not why I hired you. I hired you because someone wants me dead."

"Precisely."

But heaven help him, he wanted this woman. There was no point denying it. She was the most intriguing creature he'd ever encountered in his life. Brave. Intelligent. Witty. Independent. Unimpressed by the fact that he was a millionaire.

He set down his wine. Reaching one arm across the back of the sofa, he stroked her bare shoulder with the pad of his thumb.

To his surprise, she didn't flinch or push his hand away. All she did was wet her lips, which were moist from the wine.

"Donovan…" she said with a note of warning. "You're my client and there's—"

"Something happening between us."

He could see the gentle pulse at her neck begin to beat faster with intensity. He half expected her to get up off the sofa and walk out on him. But she didn't. For a few heated seconds, she simply sat there, allowing him to stroke a finger across the soft skin at her shoulder.

"Yes, there is something happening," she finally replied in a breathy voice that sent him hurling over the edge. "And I'm not sure what to do about it. I've never been in this situation before."

Donovan couldn't continue to fight it. Desire was burning through his body. He couldn't remember the last time he'd wanted a woman this badly.

How did she do this to him, and why?

He didn't care why. All he knew was that he had to have her. He had to satisfy the searing need to pull her close and touch her.

Slowly, cautiously, he leaned toward her. Close enough that he could smell the perfumed fragrance of her hair, feel her wine-scented breath against his face.

He hovered there, inches from her lips, waiting to see if she was in agreement, and when she made no move to pull back, he pressed his lips lightly to hers. Tentatively at first. Exploring. Seeking. Then she let out a soft little whimper of desire that fired his blood to the breaking point.

Her willing response sent a surge of lust whipping through him like a cyclone. He cupped her head in his hands and felt her lips part for him, then he swept his tongue into her hot, wet mouth and deepened the kiss.

She whimpered with pleasure again....

He inched across the sofa, so that he could take into his arms completely. She melted into him like warm butter, reaching around his shoulders and raking her fingers through his hair. She was bewitching.

He slid his hand down the side of her gown and around her curvaceous bottom, feeling his tuxedo trousers tighten over his growing arousal.

"You taste so good," he whispered at her cheek, trailing tiny kisses down to her neck while he shifted her in his arms. She tilted her head back to give him full access, and he devoured as much of her as he possibly could, kissing her bare shoulders and tasting her jawline.

Within seconds, he was easing her onto the soft cushions beneath him, reveling in the potent sensation of her hands tangled in his hair.

She wrapped her legs around his hips, and he settled himself on top of her, pulsing his hips and relising the unmitigated pleasure of her thrusting her own hips forward in return.

"Mmm," she whispered, kissing him deeply, eating at his mouth as if she'd been starving for him for days, in the same way he'd been starving for her.

A hot flame ignited inside him, followed by something resembling panic. He wasn't sure he'd be able to stop things if they went much further—and he was surprised he'd gotten *this* far. He was dangerously close to the edge of reason. The feel of this woman beneath him was like a tidal wave of undiluted, intoxicating ecstasy storming his senses. But he had to be careful. She was skittish because of their situation, and he didn't want to wreck what this could potentially become before they even got started.

Nevertheless, he slid his hand down her thigh and gathered the fabric of her skirt in his hand, carefully lifting it inch by glorious inch. Her legs were bare beneath the skirt—no stockings—and the warm softness of her smooth leg wrapped around him gave him the most exhilarating palpitations in his chest.

This was getting out of control. He wanted to make love to her right there, half-dressed on the sofa, and again afterward in his bed...

But like a predictable clock chiming midnight, signaling the end of the ball, Jocelyn squirmed and turned her face away. She pressed a palm to his chest.

"We need to stop, Donovan. We shouldn't be doing this."

He froze, immobilized while his heart continued to pump heated blood through his veins. Closing his eyes for a moment to try and gain control of his breathing, he fought the overwhelming urge to kiss her again and continue this achingly pleasurable indulgence. Then he removed his hand from the intimate place it had *almost* been, and sighed.

Jocelyn shifted slightly beneath him. He recognized her unease—and knowing a woman was uneasy beneath him was about as effective as a bucket of cold water splashing over his head.

He backed off immediately and retreated to his side of the sofa, pushing his hair back off his perspiring forehead. "Sorry about that." He paused, catching his breath. "I didn't mean to take it that far."

All he'd meant to do was kiss her....

Jocelyn pulled and tugged at the neckline of her gown to try and put herself back together. "It was my fault, too."

An awkward silence ensued.

H couldn't stand it. "Look…"

She didn't let him finish. She stood. "Maybe this was a mistake."

"No, Jocelyn—" She began to leave. "Don't go. Let's talk about this." Damn, he'd really done it now. He followed her down the hall.

"There's no point talking," she said. "I knew this was going to happen. I could see it coming, but I couldn't stop it, and that's dangerous, Donovan. I can't do my job this way. I should resign and you should find someone else."

He caught her arm. "Resign? All we did was kiss, really…."

He knew how ridiculous that sounded. It was a hell of a lot more than just a kiss.

"But it might not be just a kiss next time," she replied, "and where does it go after that? I'll be honest, I'm very attracted to you. So much so, that I'm finding it hard to keep my mind on my work. I'm supposed to be watching you constantly, but I'm not watching you the way I should be. I'm not thinking about potential danger. I'm thinking about *you*. About how badly I want to…"

Her chest was heaving.

"To *what*, Jocelyn?"

"To do what we just did."

He released her arm. "I've been thinking about it, too, and it's been getting a little crazy, but please, don't quit on me. I need you here. At least until the stalker is caught. Then…then maybe we could think about something more between us."

For a long moment she stood there, staring into his eyes, considering what he'd said.

Please don't leave, he wanted to say again and again.

But when she spoke, her voice was cool and back under control. His heart sank.

"If it's protection you need, Donovan, I don't think I'm the best person for the job. I'm sorry. I'll make the necessary arrangements for another E.P.P., and I'll stay with you until the new operative can take over, but after that, I'm gone. It's for your own safety."

She went into her room and closed the door behind her.

Donovan backed up against the wall and pinched the bridge of his nose. His chest ached, his safety the last thing on his mind as he thought about what she'd just said, and the fact that she hadn't said a word about the *us* part.

"I'm in trouble, Tess," Jocelyn said to her assistant over the phone the next morning, after she escorted Donovan safely to the O.R. She now stood in the waiting room outside. "I need some help."

"Why? What's wrong?"

Jocelyn felt some of the tension in her shoulders drain away momentarily. Tess was not only her capable and competent assistant, but her truest confidante and dear friend. She was petite and wore glasses, she was an avid reader, and she'd been with Jocelyn since she'd opened her private agency four years ago. She was a great listener who always told it like it was.

"I gave my notice to resign last night," Jocelyn said, "and Dr. Knight needs a new agent immediately."

There was a brief silence on the other end of the line. "What in the world happened? He didn't make a pass at you, did he? Like that slimy old retired senator in New Jersey?"

Jocelyn cupped her forehead with a hand. "No, it wasn't anything like that. Well, it was…I mean, he did make a pass at me, but the problem was, I was all for it. I think I might have encouraged him. I'm not sure. I can barely remember what happened. It was all such a blur. I just remember feeling swept off my feet."

Silence again. "How old is this guy?"

"He's young. Thirty-four, and gorgeous."

"You didn't tell me that."

"I know. I guess I didn't want to admit that I'd noticed."

She heard Tess take a deep breath and whistle. "As long as I've known you, you've never let this happen. Do you think you're falling for him?"

Jocelyn closed her eyes. "I don't want to admit to it, or give in to it, but…yes, I think I might be. In fact, I think I already have."

"Why don't you want to give in to it? Because he's your client? If that's the problem, we can fix it today. I can find someone else to take over, then you'll be free to go out on a date with him, or whatever."

"No, no, no, I don't *want* to go out on a date with him. I want to get as far away from him as possible. I don't want to see him again."

"Why not?"

"Because…" How could she answer that? It was personal and complicated and would take too long to explain, and it would sound ridiculous. "I just don't want to get involved with anyone right now."

She huffed. "You're crazy. And probably just scared."

Why did Tess always insist on acting as her conscience? "It's not that. I just don't have time for a relationship."

"That's crap and you know it. You're afraid to get involved with anyone because you're worried he'll be like Tom or your dad and you'll end up heartbroken."

So much for "complicated and too lengthy to explain." Tess hit the mark in one sentence.

That was Tess. Direct and to the point, even when Jocelyn wasn't quite ready to feel the point jabbing her in the behind.

Jocelyn gathered her resolve. "Donovan isn't my type. He's not looking for commitment—he said it himself over dinner last night—and from what I've learned about him, he's never had a serious, long-term relationship with anyone, at least not in his adult life. Why would I want to get involved with someone like that, when the possibility of getting my heart broken is practically a sure thing?"

"Did you ask him why?"

"Why what?"

"Why he's never had a serious relationship with anyone. Maybe he got burned once, too."

"No, I didn't ask."

"Aren't you curious?"

Yes, she was. She was curious about a lot of things.

"I really don't want to ask him, because that will only add fuel to the fire. I don't want to get any closer to him. I just want to get out of this assignment before I end up in bed with him."

"And what would be wrong with that? You're a grown-up, Jocelyn. You deserve a few guilty pleasures every now and then, and you can handle them if you want."

Jocelyn sat down on a chair. "Are you implying what I think you're implying?"

"I'm not implying anything. I'm saying it loud and clear. Do I need a megaphone? If you're attracted to him and he's attracted to you, why not steal a little enjoyment while you can? It wouldn't hurt you to ditch your professional, tough-girl attitude for a night. Especially if we find him another bodyguard. There wouldn't be any ethical problems then."

"You're saying I should have casual sex with him? I'm not good at casual sex. Call me needy, but I have a problem with the 'casual' part."

"Maybe it wouldn't end up as casual."

Jocelyn ran her fingers through her hair. "I couldn't, Tess. I'm a chicken."

"No, you're not. You're the bravest person I know. Think about what you do for a living. You can tussle with the best of 'em."

"That's different. It's my job."

"So let me get this straight. You're fearless professionally, but scared stiff personally?"

Tess was certainly blunt. It wouldn't be so bad if she wasn't completely bang on.

"Okay, okay, you get the insightful award for today," Jocelyn said, twirling a loose thread from one of her buttonholes around her finger.

"So what do you want me to do?" Tess asked.

Jocelyn considered it for a moment, then let out a deep sigh. "Try to find Dr. Knight a new E.P.P., and look into the waiting list to find me a new assignment. Preferably an out-of-town detail."

"So you're not going to take my advice." Tess didn't even try to hide the disappointment in her voice.

Jocelyn stood up to peer through one of the windows on the swinging doors to the O.R. All she could see was her own reflection, which she didn't really want to look at right now.

"Sorry, Tess. I'm not interested in taking risks with my heart. I'll be back in the office as soon as you can get me out of this. The sooner the better."

Jocelyn and Donovan were halfway home when he turned up a side street and pulled over. He shut off the car and draped an arm over the steering wheel, looking at her. "We need to talk."

Heart suddenly racing, Jocelyn looked out the windows, checking for cars that might be following them. The coast appeared to be clear, so she turned to him.

"There's nothing to talk about, Donovan. My assistant has been working all day to find you another E.P.P."

"No luck?"

"Not yet," she said, still looking out the windows. "So far, the only person available is a guy I don't trust. He's a hothead who would prefer to beat up on an attacker just to prove he's tough, when he should be shielding and evacuating his principal."

In the passenger side rearview mirror, she noticed a guy in a hoodie and ball cap approaching on the sidewalk.

"Why won't you look at me?" Donovan asked.

She kept her eyes focused on the mirror. "I'm just trying to do my job. Is your door locked?"

He checked it. "Yeah."

The guy in the hoodie walked passed them and entered a liquor store.

"There's no danger," Donovon said. "No one knows we're here."

"Let me be the judge of that."

They sat for a few seconds, while Donovan waited for her to assure herself that there were no potential dangers, then he tried again. "You don't have to quit."

Finally, she looked at him. "Like I said last night, it's for your own safety."

Donovan's gaze was direct and penetrating. "But I trust you to take care of that, even after what happened last night."

Jocelyn tried not to notice the way his jeans were pulling tight over his muscular thighs and the way her pulse was thrumming wildly in response. She tried not to think about what Tess had suggested that morning—that Jocelyn should go ahead and seek pleasure with her soon-to-be ex-client, for the mere sake of self-indulgence....

"What happened last night *shouldn't* have happened," she said, trying to purge those reckless thoughts from her mind. "It's one of the first laws of my profession—*never* get involved with a principal."

He tapped his thumb on the steering wheel and faced forward. "All right, I'll accept that, because I respect your judgment and your professionalism. If you want to resign and find another E.P.P. for me, that's fine. I'll take another E.P.P. Maybe it *would* be best."

That seemed a little too easy, but she suspected it was merely the calm before the storm.

Donovan shifted on the leather seat to face her. "Last night was incredible, Jocelyn."

Yes, it was.

"It took every ounce of self-control I possessed," he

continued, "not to follow you into your room after what happened, and pick up where we left off, when I knew I should be promising never to do it again. If I thought I could make that promise, I would try harder to convince you to stay, because I am completely willing to place my life in your hands. But I'm not that disciplined. I can't make that promise. I wanted you last night like I've never wanted any woman in my life, and that feeling's not going away. I was totally messed up today. I can't fight it, nor can I resist touching you if you're anywhere within reach."

I'm within reach now, she thought, struggling with feelings of desire and longing that were bombarding her senses and becoming impossible to ignore.

Why did he have to smell so good? Look so good? Sound so good? The moist texture of his mouth, his lips parting seductively, and the heated glimmer in his eye—it was all so tempting. Here in the car, she didn't feel like a bodyguard...she felt like a woman. A woman tingling all over. A woman struggling to resist the power of this man's appeal.

Her breaths came in short little gasps. They stared at each other for a long, pulse-pounding moment. This was insane.

"If I could resist you," he said, "I would. The unfortunate thing is, I can't."

He swayed toward her, just a little, and it was enough to break down every wall of defense she had tried to build around herself today, while he was operating on people. Her cover came crumbling down.

Donovan cupped her cheek in his hand and gazed at her for a shuddering moment before he pressed his mouth to hers.

The world spun circles as she reached her arms around his neck. All that mattered was the sensation of his hands on her body.

He whispered in her ear. "Come home with me, Jocelyn."

She nearly lost her breath.

"I want you in my bed…."

Tess's words resounded in her brain: *Why not steal a little enjoyment while you can?*

Oh, how she wanted to…

He kissed her neck and stroked her shoulders and back, then devoured her mouth again with another skillfully wet kiss that dissolved most of what was left of her resistance. She wanted this man, and she didn't care what the consequences were. Surely she could deal with her fears another day.

Then she heard laughter from somewhere outside her hazy consciousness…somewhere outside the car. She pulled back and turned. Two teenagers were standing outside her window, watching them! How long had they been there?

Realizing they'd been discovered, the youths immediately turned and ran off down the street, but the damage was done. Jocelyn had fallen down in her duties, to an unimaginable degree.

"They're gone," Donovan whispered, leaning forward to continue kissing her, but she held him back with a hand.

"No, that was a sign."

"Don't tell me you're superstitious now."

"No, I'm *awake* now, thank God. What if that had been your stalker? See how distracted I am? This is crazy, Donovan, and you know it."

He grabbed hold of the steering wheel with both hands

and tapped his forehead against it. "This *is* crazy. It's a good thing you resigned, because if you didn't, I'd have to fire you. Because I don't want you as my bodyguard anymore. I just want you in my bed."

"That can't happen." She tried to fight her still smoldering desires. "Not yet. Not now."

"But someday? Can I at least entertain some hope?"

She couldn't seem to answer right away. What just happened had spooked her, doused her with a healthy spray of reality. Her heart was racing inside her chest. Besides that, she wasn't sure she could handle a relationship with Donovan, not if it was going to blow up in her face in a month's time when he got bored because she was no longer forbidden fruit.

At her hesitation, his eyes narrowed, then he blew out a breath of air. "I need a second or two to get a hold of myself." He flicked the latch on the door and got out.

"No, wait! Donovan!" She got out, too, meeting him around the front of the vehicle and taking him by the arm. "Get back in the car. I can't be sure we're safe here."

Just then, a navy blue sedan came speeding out from behind the car that was parked to the rear of them. Jocelyn's senses exploded, and she pulled Donovan toward the sidewalk to duck down behind his car. She shielded his body with hers, just as the driver opened fire out of the passenger side window.

CHAPTER

Eight

Three bullets fired in rapid succession shattered the glass in the liquor store window, then tires squealed and the car sped off. Jocelyn tried to see the license plate, but it was too late.

Donovan rose to his feet, staring after the shooter in dismay.

"Get in the car now," Jocelyn ordered, opening the passenger side door and shoving him in. "I'll drive."

She pulled out her cell phone to call the police as she ran around the front of the vehicle. She had the emergency number on speed dial. She gave the particulars about the assailant while she got in and started the engine.

"You better buckle up," she said.

Donovan watched her squeal onto the road. "What the hell just happened?"

"We were being watched, and not only by those teenagers. Look out the rear window. Did he come back around? Are we being followed?"

"No, there's no one behind us," he replied.

She pulled a U-turn and started back in the other direction, sped onto the main road, and shifted quickly in and out of lanes.

Donovan kept one hand on the dash to brace himself. "You're quite a driver."

"Comes with training. Anybody else shifting lanes behind us?"

He turned to look. "No. It's clear."

She turned left at a busy intersection and went up a few side streets to avoid the direct route home. They finally reached his building, and Jocelyn parked out back instead of in his usual spot inside the garage. She escorted him out of the car quickly and skirted through a back entrance for which she had a key.

"I didn't even know this door was here," Donovan said. "You did your homework, didn't you?"

"Preparation is everything." She checked around corners in basement halls, moving quickly to the elevator and keeping an eye out until he was safely inside. They rode up the twenty-two floors in silence.

Jocelyn took all possible precautions entering Donovan's penthouse and locking the door behind them. She searched the place, then closed all the blinds and curtains and told Donovan to stay away from the windows.

Once she was certain they were out of immediate danger, Jocelyn led the way into the kitchen where Donovan sat on one of the stools at the center island.

"Are you all right?" she asked. "Can I get you anything? A glass of water? Or something stronger?"

"Water would be great, thanks," he replied. "Things got pretty nutty back there."

She went to fill a glass from the water cooler in the

corner. "This is obviously a very determined and dangerous stalker, and what happened today will happen again and again until he's caught, so I want to do everything I can to assist the police in their investigation." She set the glass of water down in front of him. "They're going to be here soon, so let's try again to figure out who might want to hurt you. We need to give the police something more to work with. You mentioned the grief counseling center you're working on. You don't have any plans to pave over a park or anything like that, do you?

"No, the location hasn't even been decided yet. We're still in the fund-raising stage."

"What else can you think of? Have you lost any patients lately? Could there be a grieving loved one who blames you?"

"I guess it's possible. I'm a good surgeon, but I'm not God. I've lost my share."

"Can you get me their names? Maybe the police could look into it."

He nodded.

Jocelyn called the police and asked if they'd apprehended anyone. Unfortunately, they hadn't, which was not surprising, since the assailant had sped off quickly and she hadn't identified the plate number.

She was told an officer would be there soon to ask questions, and they would be heightening the investigation.

Two hours later, after Jocelyn had dealt with the police and called Tess to report what had occurred, she found Donovan in the kitchen, cooking.

She took a seat on one of the stools. "How are you doing?"

Wearing faded jeans and a T-shirt, he stood over the

stovetop on the island, whisking something in a saucepan.

"Better," he replied. "Cooking relaxes me. Want some bacon-wrapped scallops?" He set down the whisk, opened one of the stainless steel ovens behind him, and pulled out a pan of sizzling hors d'oeuvres. He set them on a china platter, and after sticking toothpicks in them, set the platter in front of Jocelyn.

"Don't mind if I do. Oh, sweet heaven, these are delicious." Then she realized how hot they were and opened her mouth to wave a hand in front of her face. "Ow."

Donovan chuckled as he returned to his whisking. "Burn yourself? If only you would exercise such a lack of caution and restraint on the sofa with me."

She couldn't help smiling. "I'm sorry, Donovan, but you have to admit I'm right. Especially after today."

He whisked faster. "Yes, and I must say, you were pretty impressive driving my car." His eyes lifted. "You, my dear, are no debutante."

She nodded to acknowledge the compliment. "And you, sir, are an excellent cook." She popped another tender, juicy scallop into her mouth. "What are you making?"

"Grilled chicken with lemon cream sauce over angel hair pasta, and sautéed snow peas. Are you hungry?"

"I'm starved and that sounds amazing. We forgot to eat dinner, didn't we? For obvious reasons, I guess."

He tilted his head, not bothering to speak about why.

"Listen…Donovan," she said cautiously, "before we sit down to eat, I'd like to clear the air about what happened today."

His eyes lifted again. "I got shot at."

"Before that."

"You mean what we doing in the car that attracted the

voyeuristic teenagers? Yeah, that was interesting, too, wasn't it?"

"It was more than interesting," she replied, feeling like she was treading into dangerous territory, but she needing to get this out in the open, so it wouldn't happen again. "It was excruciating."

He set the saucepan aside and flicked off the burner. Slowly, sensuously, he moved toward her like a confident panther on the prowl. Her blood began to race faster through her veins.

"In what way was it excruciating? All I remember is that you saved my life today." He took her hand and pulled her gently to her feet. She stared at him for a tremulous moment while he raised her hand to his lips and kissed her knuckles.

"Don't do this to me, Donovan," she said in a low, breathy voice while she tried to fight the powerful emotions that tugged at her from all directions.

"Do what? All I'm asking is that you allow me to have hope."

She swallowed over the huge lump of anxiety in her throat. "We shouldn't be thinking about this stuff right now."

"You're the one who brought it up."

This was agonizing. "Yes, I did, because I thought we should—"

He laid a few more soft kisses on her knuckles, and the cool, lingering moisture from his lips seemed to tingle all the way down to her toes. She forgot what she was going to say. Damn him….

"You thought we should clear the air," he said for her.

"Yes." *Thank you.*

"Let's clear it, then. I promise I'll be good." He gave her hand back to her and let his own hands fall to his sides. "I'm listening."

Her heart did a few somersaults. How was it possible that he could reduce her to a stammering idiot, when a terrible thing had happened today and she'd promised herself she would be a brick wall?

"I know I said I was going to resign," she told him, "but in light of what happened today, and the fact that Tess can't seem to find anyone to replace me on such short notice, I think it's important for me to stay on for a little while."

He wet his too-inviting lips. "Ah. I suppose the next thing you're going to tell me is that the kissing has to stop."

"Precisely." She waited for his argument, prepared her rebuttals in her mind....

"Done," he said flatly.

She shook her head in disbelief. "Done? I don't believe you."

He laid his hand on his chest, looking dismayed by her lack of confidence in his ability to keep his hands to himself. "You don't trust me."

"I do trust you, it's just that...well, you haven't exactly been agreeable to my requests before now."

He considered her point. "Maybe not, but I've had some time to think about things, and I feel differently about everything tonight."

"Differently? How so?"

"I realize that in addition to the fact that I'm your client, and the fact that I was shot at today and you feel responsible, you're nervous about getting involved with me because you don't know me very well, and you're afraid I might turn out to be the player you thought I was when you first met me. A little more time together will give me the chance to prove to you that you're wrong."

She regarded him intently. "So you're going to be good? You're not going to try to tempt me or distract me?"

He touched her chin briefly. "I'm going to do my very best, hoping of course, that there will be a reward at the end."

"Like a dog treat?" she replied.

He laughed. "No." He backed away and opened the oven to serve up dinner. "Like your heart."

They ate dinner by candlelight in the formal dining room, on the shiny, polished mahogany table, and sipped sparkling, alcohol-free cranberry cocktail from crystal goblets. After the dishes were cleared, it was past ten o'clock.

"One last chance," Jocelyn said, "to cancel your surgery tomorrow morning. We could stay here and watch TV and avoid risks."

"I would if I could, but it's an important procedure. It's not something that should be postponed."

She nodded, while helping him to load the dishwasher. A few minutes later, they were yawning.

"Will you be able to sleep?" she asked.

He walked her to her bedroom door. "I doubt it."

"Do you want to stay up a little longer? We could watch a movie if it would help."

"No, I have to be in the O.R. at 6:00 a.m. I should at least try to get some shut-eye."

"All right. Well, don't worry. I'm here, and remember I

sleep with one eye open, the monitor's on, and your new alarm system is second to none. You'll be fine tonight."

He settled one broad shoulder against her doorjamb, and relaxed there, just looking at her. "Will I?"

Jocelyn's insides began to quiver. "Of course," she replied, even though she knew he was referring to another kind of agitation. The kind that went hand in hand with temptation.

His voice was calm and soothing after the madness of the day. "I'm sure you're right."

Still, he remained at her door, gazing into her eyes, then down at her lips, back up at her eyes again.

"You're hovering," she said in a playful tone. "Remember what you promised."

"I promised I wouldn't kiss you. I didn't promise I wouldn't look at you. It's not easy to pry my eyes away, you know."

"Well, you'd better if you're going to be able to keep them open during surgery in the morning."

He visibly snapped himself out of it, and stepped away from the doorjamb. "You're right, you're right. I should go." He started to back away. "Thanks, Jocelyn."

"For what?"

He paused in the hall. "For being here."

"It's my job."

"No, it's more than that. You make me feel..." He shrugged, starting to back away again. "This is weird. I've never been so happy to have a woman stay overnight, when there wasn't any chance of you-know-what."

"Parcheesi?"

He laughed. "Is that what they call it these days?"

"God only knows."

He laughed again, still backing away. "You're adorable."

Jocelyn began to close her door. "Good night, Doctor."

"You're breaking my heart."

"And you're breaking a promise. Good night," she repeated, closing her door until it clicked, but remaining there with her ear against it, just to hear the sound of his footfalls until they disappeared into his room.

~⊘~

At 3:00 a.m., Jocelyn awoke to a knock at her door. "Yes?"

Donovan answered from the hall. "Are you awake?"

Her shoulders heaved with a sigh, and she climbed out of bed and opened the door to find him standing there looking sleepy, disheveled and shirtless, with nothing on but a pair of black pajama bottoms.

"I woke you, didn't I?" he asked.

"It's okay. I had to get up to answer the knock at my door anyway."

He smiled, and she wasn't quite sure how she'd managed to speak, with that smooth, muscular chest at eye level. Her senses were in a jumbled mess.

She noticed that his eyes were bloodshot. "Can't sleep?"

"Not a wink so far. I think it was everything that happened today. I'm still wired."

"I know the feeling. What can I do? Want some hot milk or something?"

"Hot milk? What, am I twelve?"

"You don't drink hot milk?"

He raised his eyebrows and shook his head. "I didn't think *anybody* drank hot milk anymore. Everybody wants pills."

"Not me. Pills make me fuzzy headed in the morning." She started toward the kitchen. "Come on, I'll make you some."

They both walked barefoot to the kitchen and turned on the lights. Jocelyn poured some milk into a mug and stuck it in the microwave. While the appliance hummed, she explained the hot milk technique.

"If you want it to work, you have to make sure you close your eyes as soon as the sleepy feeling kicks in, because if you don't, you'll miss it. It's like a wave you have to catch. So you shouldn't drink it in the living room, because then you'll have to get up and go to bed, and that alone might make you miss the wave. Drink it in bed."

"I see. Sounds like you've got it down to a science."

"I do." The microwave beeped, and she removed the steaming cup and stirred it with a spoon. "Here you go."

He accepted the cup and smelled it. "Hot milk. Hmm."

She put her hand on his back to usher him back to bed, and the warm feel of his well-toned muscles beneath her fingertips sent shivers up and down her spine. She tried to ignore them, but it was no use. She gave up trying, and resolved to go back to her own bed ASAP.

They reached his bedroom, and she hesitated for a fraction of a second before going with him inside. She'd never escorted a principal to bed before—and certainly not a principal who looked like Donovan, bare-chested and devastatingly masculine in nothing but his drawstring pajama bottoms. It would never have seemed appropriate with any of her previous clients, nor had any of them ever attempted to push the boundaries like Donovan did.

Still, his comfort and safety were her concern, so she entered the room. "You'll be all right now?" she asked, pausing at the bottom of the king-sized bed while he set the mug on his side table and climbed in.

"I don't know. It depends on the hot milk."

She was about to say good-night, when he gestured toward the chair in the corner. "Have a seat. Stay and talk to me for a few minutes. Tell me something personal."

She swallowed nervously. "Like what?"

"I don't know. Like what kind of person you were in high school. Were you popular—you know, the student council type, the prom queen—or did you hang out with the theater crowd?"

Jocelyn moved to the chair and sat down. "I wasn't anything. I just went to class, got average grades, had a few friends I hung out with most of the time."

"Your basic invisible kid," he said, a little too perceptibly, "ignored for being normal. Did you have any boyfriends? Or was the social climbing med student your one and only true love?"

"No, I didn't have any boyfriends in high school," she replied, somewhat grudgingly. "I had a couple of guys who were friends, and we hung out some times, but I didn't even go to the prom. None of us did. Looking back on it, maybe we were geeks. I was a bit of a loner. Still am."

"But why? You're gorgeous and funny. You should have been snapped up by now."

She sat forward. "It's simpler this way. I've gotten used to living alone and I like to focus all my energy on work. I don't have to worry about disappointing anyone when I don't come home for weeks on end. But hey, who are you to point the finger, Mr. Single-Man."

He took the first sip of his milk. "Point taken, but I've had some really good excuses. First it was med school, which kept me busy constantly, then there were years of residencies, where I was sleep-deprived and stressed out most of the time. There was no time for a relationship."

"What about now?" she asked, remembering how Tess had pushed to ask this very question. "You've been here in Chicago for a couple of years, and you appear to have an active social life. You go to the theater and you have women calling you to ask you out. Have you had any long term relationships?"

He took another sip. "Not really."

"Who's fault is that?"

He gave her a playful look. "It couldn't be mine. I'm perfect, don't ya know."

Jocelyn chuckled.

"Seriously though," he continued, taking another sip from his mug, "I know I haven't seemed like much of a family guy, and maybe I'm not. I've been on my own for a long time."

"You must have some family. Brothers? Sisters?"

He shook his head. "I'm an only child. Not that my parents ever intended it to be that way. They died when I was two."

She felt a stirring of grief. "I'm so sorry. I didn't know. I mean, I knew they weren't alive, but I didn't know when you lost them. What happened?"

He gazed down at his mug as he spoke. "Car accident. I was in the back seat, and we hit a patch of ice and went over a low cliff. Somehow I survived, and someone heard me crying the next morning. A woman found me still in the car seat, suffering symptoms of exposure. My parents had been dead all night. It's a miracle I survived."

"Oh, my God. Do you remember any of it?"

He shook his head. "No. I barely remember my parents, though my grandmother raised me and she always talked about them, showed me pictures to help me remember. She was good to me. She died when I was seventeen and I received my inheritance then, which—aside from a small monthly allowance for my upbringing—had been held in trust. This penthouse was part of it. My parents had bought it together when they married, and they'd intended to spend their lives here. I lived in it with them when I was very small, before they died. Then, like the rest of the estate, it was held in trust. So you see, I didn't always have money, and I didn't ask for it, nor do I consider it a part of who I am. I'd give it all away this minute to have had my parents back."

Jocelyn's whole body ached with empathy for Donovan's loss. She had already realized that he wasn't shallow. This only reconfirmed it. "I had no idea. What about becoming a doctor? When did you decide to do that?"

"I always knew that's what I wanted to do. Unlike your ex, it wasn't because I wanted a fancy penthouse or expensive car. I think it was because I wanted to feel like I had some control over saving people's lives, because I sure as hell felt powerless all my life, having lost my parents. I didn't know why I was so lucky to be spared, and I wanted to give something back and make my survival worthwhile. So I used part of the inheritance to put myself through medical school. When I was finished my residencies, that's when I came back here to live. It was kind of strange—like coming home, even though I barely remember living here when I was little." He was quiet for a moment. "Too bad air bags weren't standard back then. They might have lived."

Jocelyn got up and went to sit beside him on the bed.

She reached forward and stroked the hair back from his forehead, then cupped his cheek with her hand. "I'm so sorry that happened to you."

"Me, too. From what I heard, my parents were wonderful people."

She rubbed his forehead again. "Is that why you're trying to raise money for the grief counseling center for kids?"

"Yeah. I know what it can do to a child. The fear and the grief, the abandonment issues and survivor guilt."

He finished the last of his hot milk and sat forward to set the mug on his side table. When he reached across, she saw there was not only a scar on his shoulder—which she had noticed when they'd gone running that first day—but more scars under his arm, along his ribs.

She reached out to touch them while he was still leaning. "That's two car accidents you've been in. These look like they were serious."

He raised his arm to inspect them himself. "They've healed nicely though, don't you think?"

"I guess so." She continued to touch them, feeling the warmth of his skin, wanting desperately to rub away the pain he must have suffered, both as a child, and a year ago when he'd been hit by that other car. "You said a woman went through a red light and rammed you?"

"Yeah."

"Did she live?"

"No. She wasn't wearing a seat belt."

Jocelyn considered that. "Was she drunk?"

"No. Apparently she and her husband just had a fight, and she was pretty messed up."

Jocelyn continued to touch the scars, tilting her head to

the side as she stared down at them. "What was the date of the accident?"

He told her.

"That's exactly a year to the day before the intruder broke into your house and left you the letter. You don't suppose…"

Donovan sat forward. "That the husband has it out for me?"

"It's a possibility." Jocelyn went to get her phone. "I'll leave a voice mail message with the cop who was here today and have him check it out."

She made the phone call from the kitchen, then returned to Donovan's bedroom. She was about to tell him not to think about it anymore, to try and get some sleep, but she didn't have to.

She approached the bed. His eyes were closed, his breathing deep and heavy.

"See? Hot milk works." She bent forward and placed a gentle kiss on his forehead.

She pulled the covers up over his legs and watched him for a moment, gazing at the perfection of his face—the strong line of his jaw, the straightness of his nose, the beauty of his eyes, even when they were closed.

He was handsome, yes, but there was so much more to him than that, she thought, her heart still aching from what he'd told her about his parents.

She imagined him making the decision to start a grief counseling clinic for children. He must have spent his whole life pondering and mulling over his childhood and upbringing, longing for what had been taken from him, and wishing someone had been able to ease the pain. Now, he wanted to help other children, to help ease *their* pain.

Jocelyn swallowed over a lump in her throat. There was a very big heart in there, she realized, gazing down at Donovan's chest, fighting the urge to lay her hand on his skin and feel his heart beating. It was a fragile, wounded heart that had never found the courage to love anyone.

It was no wonder. *I know what it can do to a child. The fears and the grief the abandonment issues...*

She suddenly understood what he'd meant earlier that night, when he'd said he wanted to prove that he wasn't a playboy. He obviously had a deep understanding of the damage that could be done when someone loved with their whole heart, and then suffered loss. He wasn't frivolous or cavalier about relationships.

Feeling suddenly sleepy, Jocelyn pulled the covers up to Donovan's shoulders and turned from the room. Something tugged inside her—a determination that shot through her like a rocket. A deep and soulful desire to protect this man, no matter what it took, no matter how long.

Never in her career had she ever experienced anything quite like it.

The next night, they returned home to Donovan's penthouse after a long, stressful day at the hospital. Stressful for Donovan, because of the two back-to-back surgeries, and stressful for Jocelyn, who didn't relax or let down her guard, even for a minute, grilling everyone and anyone who wanted to get within ten paces of Donovan, and constantly watching over her shoulder. Realizing her limitations, she had called Tess to look into retaining a few more operatives to make this a team detail and increase security temporarily, at least until they gained some leads on the stalker.

Shortly after they entered the penthouse, the phone rang.

"I'll get it." Jocelyn answered the telephone in the front hall. "Hello? Sergeant O'Reilly, have you learned anything?"

Donovan approached, watching her and waiting, curious about what the police had managed to discover during the day.

"I see." She met Donovan's gaze. "Yes. We were lucky. I'm not sure yet. Yes, I'll do that. Thank you for letting me know." She hung up the phone.

"What happened?" Donovan asked.

Jocelyn moved toward him and placed her hand on his arm. "You won't believe what I'm going to tell you. Maybe we should go and sit down."

She led the way into the living room, where they both sat on the sofa. Jocelyn took Donovan's hand in hers, and held it. "The man whose wife died in that car accident is very likely the man who's stalking you. His name is Ben Cohen."

Donovan frowned at her. "How do the police know?"

"Because after I gave them the information, they went to his apartment to question him. He wasn't there, but the landlady told them some things that gave them enough reason to get a search warrant, and when they got inside, they found pictures of you on his wall, newspaper articles about the accident, pictures of your smashed SUV, among other things."

"Did they arrest him?"

"That's the problem. He wasn't there, and he hadn't been there for a while. The landlady said a week or two. The police don't know where he is. He hasn't been to work in a week, either. He hasn't even called in sick."

"It sounds like he *wants* people to know he's the one."

"Yes, which makes him all the more dangerous, because he has no fear. This is a personal vendetta for him, and he doesn't care about the consequences. He doesn't seem to care that he's going to lose his job or his apartment, and most likely go to prison."

Donovan cupped his forehead in his hand and squeezed his pounding temples. "The accident wasn't even my fault. *She* was the one who ran the red light."

"I know, but he's obviously not rational. He wants someone to blame, and from what the police found in his apartment, he has an axe to grind with rich people. And he hates SUV's. He thinks they're an environmental hazard that will destroy the world, and rich people don't care. And then *your* SUV killed his wife."

"This is crazy." Donovan stood up and paced around the living room. "I didn't get an SUV to kill people. I got it because it was good in the snow and in my line of work—trying to *save* people—I can't afford to get stuck on the way to the hospital."

"I know, I know," Jocelyn said, rising to her feet and going to his side. "None of this is your fault. He's insane, but at least we know who he is and the police are keeping an eye out for him. They'll catch him. It won't take long."

"But in the meantime?" Donovan turned to her. "How am I supposed to go about my life, while I'm looking over my shoulder, waiting to get shot at again?"

She took his hand in hers. "You're not supposed to go about your life, not if I have any say about it."

He frowned. "What are you suggesting?"

"It's my job to protect you, Donovan, and the risk-level—now that we know what's going on—has skyrocketed in the past twenty-four hours. You can't continue to do the things you normally do, because he's been watching, waiting for the chance to strike—like yesterday on the sidewalk. I don't want you to be a sitting duck. I need to take you away from here."

"I can't tell you where I'm going," Donovan said to his friend, Dr. Mark Reeves, over the phone, "because I don't know. She won't tell me."

"I had no idea it would get this serious," Mark said. "I

half thought the intruder was a burglar, like the police wanted to believe, and I thought maybe the letter was unconnected. Or maybe I was just hoping."

"Look, don't worry," Donovan replied. "Jocelyn is a pro. She knows what she's doing and I have total confidence in her. On that note, thanks for sending her my way."

"You're welcome. So you really don't know where you're going?"

Donovan sighed. "All I know is that she's going to take me some place where no one will find us."

Mark paused. "You're not just making this up, are you? So you can take off with her on a wild Jamaican weekend while I cover your patients?"

Donovan rolled his eyes. "No, Mark."

"Don't fault me. A guy can't help but be curious. She's not unattractive, you know. And I saw the way you looked at each other at the hospital the other day. There's got to be something going on."

The direction of the conversation unnerved Donovan suddenly. He tried to laugh it off. "Mark, you really need to get a life. I gotta go."

"Wait, why won't you tell me anything?"

Donovan considered the question for a moment. "My kiss-and-tell days are over. Look...thanks for covering my patients. I'll see you when I get back."

Donovan hung up the phone, anxious to get on the road with Jocelyn, to wherever they were going. He was curious about that, too.

~ⓒ

After a long, careful trip out of Chicago in a rented car

under Tess's name, Jocelyn turned left onto a winding, woodsy road that led to the cabin. No one would ever be able to trace them there, and it had the added benefit of being familiar to Jocelyn, who had come here twice before. It was the perfect hideout.

They drove through the shady woods for a few miles, churning up dust on the dry road while rays of sunshine gleamed like dappled light through the trees.

Donovan looked out the window. "This is really isolated. You're sure we'll be safe here?"

Safe from the stalker, yes. Safe from her growing attraction to Donovan? Not likely, considering this was probably the most romantic place on earth.

"Positive." She tried to sound confident and ignore her personal feelings. "No one knows where we are, and I took the necessary precautions when we left the city."

They finally pulled up in front of a cedar, prow-fronted cabin overlooking a lake, with huge floor-to-ceiling windows and a multilevel deck with patio furniture, a round table with a sun umbrella and a barbecue. Rich green grass went all the way down to the water, where a small cruiser was tied up at a private wharf.

"This is beautiful," Donovan said. "You sure know how to pick a nice spot to be hiding out in."

"Well, I figured if we're going to be forced to leave town and be inconvenienced by Cohen, we might as well be comfortable, and maybe even enjoy ourselves."

Enjoy ourselves. She shouldn't have said that. It evoked all kinds of inappropriate thoughts.

Jocelyn turned off the car. The silence was astonishing. All they could hear was a single bird chirping, and the sound of a light breeze whispering through the pines and leafy elms.

Donovan stared at the cabin. "You've been here before?"

"Twice, yes. Wait till you see the inside."

They opened their doors and breathed in the clean scent of the woods, then stepped onto a carpet of soft, brown pine needles in the driveway. Fetching their bags out of the trunk, they made their way up to the door, where the key and a welcome note from the owners were waiting for them in the wooden mailbox. Jocelyn opened the door and let Donovan enter first, before following him inside.

Nothing had changed since the last time she'd been here. Everything was rustic pine—the kitchen table and chairs, the hutch full of china, the plank floor and the walls, as well as the honey-pine ceiling, supported by solid cedar timbers.

"Wow," Donovan said, looking up at the cathedral ceiling in the great room and the monstrous, gray stone fireplace. "Looks like we're going to get that vacation we've both been needing. How long do we get to stay?"

She set down her bag. "That depends on how long it takes the police to find Cohen. Could be twenty-four hours, could be a month."

"Let's hope it's a month. Though I doubt the hospital would be happy about that."

Jocelyn locked the door behind them. "Come on, I'll show you the bedrooms."

She picked up her bag and led the way across the open concept kitchen and living area, to the bedroom on the ground floor. A four-poster pine bed stood against the wall. White wicker furniture was arranged in a corner beside the glass sliding doors that led out onto a deck.

"I'll take this room," she said, then led him across to the

other side of the cabin, where they climbed stairs to a loft.

The master suite had its own balcony and private bath, as well as a skylight over the bed.

Donovan set down his bag. "That'll be nice for stargazing."

"For sure. You'll be comfortable enough here?"

He walked to the bed and sat down. "I think so." They regarded each other steadily for a few seconds, then he stood up again. "Do you mind if I ask...have you brought other clients here? Or do you just come here for pleasure? You said you haven't had a vacation in a while."

Jocelyn sighed, wishing she didn't feel so inclined to answer his personal questions, but ever since the night in his bedroom, when he told her about his past and she told him things about her personal life, she'd felt more connected to him—like she was talking to a friend she'd known for years.

"I wouldn't exactly call it pleasure," she replied, "but it wasn't for work, either."

He sauntered toward her. "Now you've got me curious."

Her pulse began to race as he approached, stopping in front of her, close enough that she could smell his musky male scent. She realized this was going to be a very difficult assignment over the next few days.

"All right, I'll tell you. I came here the first time with my mother when I was fourteen, just after my father left us. She wanted to get away, so she wouldn't have to answer the phone and explain to everyone what happened. We stayed for two weeks. Then I came back alone, years later, after Tom and I broke up."

Donovan stared at her for a moment. "So this place doesn't exactly have *pleasant* memories for you."

She shook her head.

"Why did you choose it?"

"Because it was the safest place I knew, and I'd basically already done the advance. I know the layout of the property and the inside of the cabin like the back of my hand."

"Always a professional," he said.

"I try."

He gazed at her pensively for a few more seconds, then thankfully dropped the subject. She had the feeling, however, that it would come up again at some point.

"Want to get the groceries out of the car?" he asked.

"Sure." Jocelyn led the way down the stairs.

They brought in the food—a week's supply that Tess had picked up for them and delivered just before they left Chicago in the middle of the night. They stowed it away in the fridge and cupboards.

"What would you like for dinner tonight?" Donovan asked, checking out the cooking utensils in the drawers. "I don't want to influence you, but I make a perfect barbecued steak."

"Sounds great."

If his steak was half as good as his chicken and lemon sauce, and he continued to be such an enjoyable dinner companion, Jocelyn was going to find it very difficult to remember that she was not here for pleasure. Epicurean or otherwise.

She was here to do a job, and keep this man alive.

⁓⊘

That evening after dinner, they walked down to the beach. The water was calm, except for tiny, circular ripples from fish bobbing at the surface. The sun was setting just beyond the tree line on the other side of the lake.

It was a hot night, so Jocelyn had changed into a black T-shirt and khaki walking shorts with Nike sandals, but Donovan still wore his jeans. Jocelyn spread a blanket on the sand.

"Listen to the crickets," he said. "What a night. This is unbelievable."

He began to unbutton his shirt.

"What are you doing?"

He shrugged out of it, then hopped on one foot while he pulled off a shoe. "I'm checking out the lake."

"Are you wearing a swimsuit under those jeans?" she asked, trying not to stare at the sheer magnificence of his bare chest in the glimmering twilight.

"Nope." He pulled off the other shoe.

"Hold on a second!" Jocelyn blurted out, holding up a hand. "You can't do that here!"

"Why not? There's no one around."

"*I'm* around, and I don't particularly want to see your—"

Good heavens.

He pulled down his jeans, and she caught a flash of his bare hip just before she shut her eyes and whirled around to face the other direction. The next thing she heard was the sound of bare feet running onto the wharf and a huge, resounding splash.

Jocelyn opened her eyes, turned and looked down at Donovan's clothes on the blanket at her feet.

All of them.

Right down to the baby blue boxers.

She walked to the edge of the wharf just as Donovan resurfaced. "The water's great!" He flipped his wet hair back off his face. He was one beautiful man. "You should come in."

"I will most certainly *not* come in."

He laughed. "Why not? There's no one here but us. Relax for once. Just for a minute."

She shook her head at him. "I've said it before and I'll say it again—that's precisely when something will happen—as soon as I let down my guard. You've hired me to do a job, and I intend to do it. I'll just watch." She glanced around the lake, scanning carefully in all directions.

"Have it your way."

He dove under the water, and she saw more than she wanted to see—a tight, muscular bare behind to die for. Nervous butterflies invaded her belly.

Was he trying to drive her mad on purpose? She cupped her forehead in her hand and shut her eyes again.

Feeling slightly desperate, she glanced all around, looking for anybody who might suddenly appear. The owners, perhaps? A lost hiker? Of course there was no one, so she looked back down at Donovan, frolicking in the water and driving her insane with a mixture of exasperation and desire to join him.

He treaded water and looked up at her with a tempting smile. "Sure you won't change your mind?"

"I'm sure." But she wasn't sure. What she really wanted to do was dive into that lake and cool off. Because she was perspiring heavily now.

"I know you want to," he said teasingly, still treading water. "Just five minutes. You said yourself that no one could possibly know we're here. Why can't you just enjoy yourself?"

Now he was making her feel like a prude. A boring old stick-in-the-mud.

Which she was. When was the last time she truly enjoyed herself? Or went out on a date that didn't involve work? When had she laughed, outside of these last few days with Donovan?

"I'd like to, but…"

"No more buts. Just dive in. I'll even turn around while you get undressed."

She stood for a few seconds, considering it while Donovan continued to tread water with his back to her. Oh, what would it hurt? Five minutes. He was right. She'd done her job and done it well. No one could possibly find them here.

"All right," she said reluctantly, pulling her T-shirt off over her head. "But I'm not getting naked. I'm wearing undergarments that are perfectly respectable for swimming."

She was glad she'd worn the new black bra and matching panties that Doris had picked out for her, to go with the black dress. It almost looked like a real bikini.

He laughed. "Whatever floats your boat."

Shaking her head, Jocelyn stepped out of her shorts and folded everything neatly in a pile. She walked to the edge of the wharf.

"Okay, you can look now." She reached her arms out in front of her, paused, then did a double forward flip through the air into the water.

As soon as she surfaced, she heard Donovan clapping and whooping. "That was amazing! What, you were an Olympic diver in your past life?"

She rubbed the water from her eyes. "No, but I was on the swim team in college."

"You do everything well, don't you?" He swam closer.

She shrugged, trying not to think about the fact that he

was completely naked in the water, not two feet away from her now, and she was in her underwear. If she moved any closer, she'd be able to touch him.

Lord, she wanted to. Her body was practically humming with the desire to wrap her arms around his neck. To feel his cheek next to hers.

She wanted to let go of all her inhibitions—just this once—and do what Tess had suggested. Take advantage of this romantic summer night with the most handsome man on the planet....

She took a deep breath and dunked her head, still trying to cool off, but realizing it was hopeless and she might as well resign herself to a painful, heated lust for the next half hour or so.

They dipped and dove and swam around each other as the sun disappeared behind the trees. The sensual feel of the cool water on Jocelyn's skin was pure heaven.

After a few minutes, Donovan came closer, treading water. "I have a goal," he said. "Concerning you."

She managed to keep her breathing steady as she spoke. "What is it? You're not going to teach me to cook, are you?"

"No."

"To perform heart surgery on a raccoon?"

He laughed. "No."

"What then?"

Donovan's eyes smoldered with determination. "I want to make our time here...*pleasant* for you."

As she gazed into his glimmering eyes, she couldn't think of a single thing to say. She wasn't quite sure what he was suggesting, though something about it made her feel all warm and gooey inside.

Thankfully he elaborated. "The last two times you were

here were some of the worst times in your life. This is a beautiful place, and you should have fond memories of it."

Beginning to understand his meaning, she slicked her wet hair back. "You mean you want to help me cleanse the cabin of its past?"

"In a matter of speaking, yes."

She was now treading water, very close to Donovan. "Why?"

He slowly blinked. "Because you've done a lot to help me, and I just want to see you smile."

"You've seen me smile."

"Not often."

The way he was looking at her now—with tenderness and caring—it was softening all her female powers of resistance.

She grinned at him. "That fortune cookie was right. You do like to fix things. It's why you want to open that grief counseling center to help children. It's why you became a heart surgeon. It's why you want to work on me now."

"I don't want to *work* on you," he replied.

"Yes, you do, but I'm not complaining. It's nice. No one's ever wanted to make me happy before. They always wanted to use me for *their* happiness. But what about you, Donovan? You deserve happiness, too. Maybe I should also have a goal while we're here."

They swam in circles around each other. "What are you suggesting?" His voice was a low murmur.

It was almost completely dark by now. The moon was low in the sky. Stars were beginning to twinkle. "I'm suggesting that if you feel the need to do something nice for me, I should do something nice for you in return."

He paused, treading water. "And how do you intend to do that?"

She swam closer until she was nose-to-nose with him in the water. The magic of the night enveloped her. A brief shiver rippled through her body, followed by a wave of heady excitement.

She was tired of being the consummate professional, day in and day out, every minute of her life. For once, she just wanted to be a woman.

"Like this." Then she slowly pressed her lips to his.

CHAPTER

Ten

T he kiss was hot and wet and way overdue, Jocelyn thought, as she stroked her hands over Donovan's dripping hair and settled them on his shoulders. He folded her into his strong embrace, and in response, she let go of her reserve and wrapped her legs around him.

Before she knew what was happening, she was spinning slowly through the water, and he was carrying her toward shore.

They emerged out of the water onto the beach. Kissing deeply and passionately, they reached the blanket and Donovan sank easily to his knees. He laid Jocelyn on her back and came down smoothly on top of her.

She tipped her head back and sighed, while he kissed her neck and shoulders and made her feel free and out of control with desire.

She could hardly believe this was happening—that this beautiful man was kissing her and loving her outdoors beneath a star-speckled sky.

"Donovan, this is crazy," she whispered. "What if someone sees us?"

His discerning gaze scanned the yard around them. "There's no one here."

Satisfied that he had dispelled her concerns, Donovan pressed his mouth to hers again and slid his hand down the side of her body, over the curve of her hip. "Are you cold?" he whispered in her ear, his hot breath sending wonderful little shivers down her spine.

"No, I'm burning up."

His gaze found hers and he smiled—warm, open and adoring. "Then I'll try to cool you down, though it won't be easy, considering I'm on fire, too."

He was still smiling when he kissed her again, and she pulled him tight against her, wanting to give him the same kind of pleasure he was giving her. Soon it wasn't enough, and she wanted more. She wanted to feel him inside her. She was tired of holding back.

Jocelyn wiggled out of her panties and slid them off. She sat up, gently pushed him onto his back on the blanket, and straddled him. "I just want to make sure you know that this is me making *you* happy tonight, and not the other way around."

He laughed, and took her hips in his hands and shifted slightly beneath her. "I see. You're trying to set this up so that I *owe* you."

"Absolutely. And I'll expect payback as soon as you're able."

He smiled and filled her with a tantalizing sweetness that sent her passions soaring, then he pushed her hair back from her face and pulled her down for another soul-reaching kiss.

Their bodies moved together in the moonlight, while Jocelyn's thoughts seemed to come to her on a floating cloud. How long had it been since she'd made love to someone?

Years…. Not since Tom, and quite frankly, it had never been like this. Tonight she was overcome. She felt cared for and protected, all of which was unfamiliar, for it seemed she was always on the other end of that spectrum. This was pure bliss.

She plunged herself into the rapture, and afterward—weak and out of breath—she collapsed on top of Donovan. He held her for a few minutes, then rolled her over onto her back. She gazed up at him adoringly, while the moon shone brightly overhead.

He leaned on one elbow and looked down at her, caressing her face, playing with her hair. "What changed your mind about this?"

She took a moment to think about that. "It wasn't really a rational decision. If I was being rational, I wouldn't be here like this, naked and completely vulnerable on a beach with you. It was more of a surrender. I just couldn't fight it anymore."

"*It* being…?"

She ran her fingers through his hair. "The way I'm feeling about you. The way you make me remember that I'm a woman with needs and desires."

"You're *all* woman, Jocelyn, and you're a real turn-on. Don't ever forget that. And I'm glad you're here with me."

She smiled up at him, wishing this moment could last forever, but knowing that it couldn't. She had to go back to being on guard very soon. She couldn't relax like this much longer. Or at least not without some professional safety precautions.

~⊘

Later that evening, after Donovan took a shower and changed, he went downstairs to make popcorn. He could hear the shower still running in Jocelyn's bathroom, so he took his time getting things ready—lighting some candles, pouring their drinks, fluffing up the pillows on the blue chintz sofa.

She was taking a long time in the shower, he thought to himself as he opened the popcorn jar and went searching for cooking oil. He hoped she wouldn't regret what they'd done. He certainly didn't. In fact, he'd never been so ecstatic about making love to a woman before. Then again, he'd never known a woman quite like Jocelyn.

He found the oil and poured some into the heavy pot he'd set on the stove, then stood back and stared down at it while he waited for it to heat up.

What was it about her that drove him so mad with desire? He wanted her, but more than just sexually. He wanted to be close to her—to know everything about her childhood and her adulthood and her job and her personal life, and he wanted to share those things about himself with her as well.

His insides stirred with an odd mixture of elation and trepidation. Was this love, or the beginnings of it?

Maybe it was, but how could he know for sure? He'd never loved a woman before. He'd felt lust for them, certainly, and he'd been infatuated with girlfriends during high school and med school, but never had he wanted to make the kinds of promises that would last forever, or trust a woman with his heart. He'd never felt a desire to spend every waking minute of every day with any woman from his past.

Until now. It was different with Jocelyn.

Maybe it was her down-to-earth nature. She didn't put on any false airs. She was real, and he felt like he knew her as deeply as he knew himself.

An unfamiliar feeling of contentment moved through him, and he exhaled a breath. It was a pleasant sensation, and he smiled.

A half a second later, something deep inside him warned him to be careful. He'd never trusted anyone with his heart before, and it wasn't easy to let go of years of independence. There was also the fear that a relationship with Jocelyn might eventually go sour. How the hell would he handle it if she disappeared from his life?

He'd been there before.

In fact, he'd *always* been there. Being alone was part of his identity, even when he was with other people.

Except for Jocelyn.

His bodyguard.

Was *that* why he felt able to trust her in ways he never trusted other women? Because she was sworn to protect him, and he believed that she would, no matter what? She had thrown her body on top of him when bullets started flying in Chicago. He'd never be able to forget that.

But she was obligated to be his bodyguard, and he knew she wouldn't shirk her responsibilities in order to become his full-time lover. She'd made it clear that she didn't like to get involved with clients, nor was she looking for a committed relationship. How many times had she told him that she didn't need anything in her life outside of her work?

Feeling suddenly uncertain about what was happening between them and where it might lead, he poured the popcorn kernels into the pot and covered it.

Jocelyn came out of her room just then, wearing a white terry cloth bathrobe and thick white socks that pooled around her ankles. She was rubbing a towel over her wet hair.

Donovan was mesmerized. "How is it possible that you can look that good, just coming out of the shower?"

She gave him the sparkling smile he'd been waiting to see. It almost knocked him backward into the stove.

"You're a charmer." She moved toward him and kissed him on the cheek, but he pulled her close for a deeper kiss on the mouth. He wanted to make love to her again, right then and there.

"What's cooking?" she asked.

"Popcorn."

She glanced at the pot. "You're making it on the stove? What a treat."

"*You're* the treat," he replied, enjoying the way she winked flirtatiously at him, then turned around and moved into the living room.

He returned his attention to the stove and shook the pot continuously until a movie-theater aroma filled the cabin and the popcorn raised the lid off the pot. Donovan poured the popcorn into a bowl, then he melted butter to drizzle over the top.

Jocelyn was sitting on the sofa, twirling a lock of her hair around a finger, waiting for him. As soon as he set the bowl down on the coffee table, she pulled her legs up under her.

"Donovan, we really should talk about what happened between us tonight."

He was about to sit down, but found himself frozen on the spot. "Let me guess. You're about to tell me that it can't happen again."

She reached up and took hold of his hand. "Please, just sit down with me."

He did as she asked, though he would have preferred to go back to the way he'd felt five minutes ago when she'd given him that dazzling smile and kissed him in the kitchen.

"It sounds like you did some thinking while you were in the shower," he said.

"Yes, I did, and I think we need to set out some parameters."

"Parameters?" Damn, he wasn't ready for the disappearing act yet. He still wanted more. "I don't like the sound of that."

"I know, but it's important, considering the situation. I can't risk your safety."

He leaned forward and rested his elbows on his knees. "Look, I know you feel like you lost control down there at the lake, and I'm sorry if I pressured you into coming in for a swim, but you have to admit, what happened because of it was pretty great."

She squeezed his hand and smiled. "I'm not denying that at all. It was incredible."

At least she was giving him that.

"We can manage this," he said. "You told me that we're safe here, that it's low-risk. The chances of anyone finding us are—"

She touched a finger to his lips to hush him. "You don't have to talk me into anything. I had a great time, too, and I want to do it again. I have every intention of it, actually."

His whole body flooded with relief, followed by heat and desire. "I just want to make sure I heard you correctly. You just said…"

"Yes. I did do some thinking in the shower, and I decided that because this is a low-risk detail at the moment, and since we've already broken the ice, so to speak, that we should set out some parameters to make sure we can make love again, and still exercise caution." She pointed at the lake. "What we did down there? That was definitely *not* cautious."

"So, you're saying…"

"I'm saying I think we should stick to your bedroom from now on. With the door locked and the monitor on."

Donovan felt all the tension drain out of his shoulders. It was replaced by another type of tension—the kind that required a very satisfying cure.

He leaned back on the sofa and raked his fingers through his hair, and sighed. "Thank God."

Jocelyn laughed. "What, did you think I was going to torture you for the next few days? Torture both of us?"

He shook his head. "I don't know what I thought."

She swayed toward him and took his face in her hands. "What happened down at the lake was amazing, and I have no regrets. We're here in this beautiful spot, I'm attracted to you and you seem to be attracted to me. We're both adults, so I don't see why we shouldn't enjoy each other, as long as we act responsibly and take precautions."

She was making it sound like a casual, temporary fling.

A part of him wanted to talk her out of that—to convince her that they could be so much more than that, if they wanted to be.

But in light of the uncertainty he still felt about how

willing he was to risk his own heart, he decided it would be best to just nod and say yes. She was offering him a few days of no-strings-attached lovemaking. Maybe it was all she could give. For all he knew, maybe it was all *he* could give. He couldn't possibly predict, because this was uncharted territory.

This was a good thing, he decided, smiling at her and leaning in for a kiss. It would give them both time to get to know each other, without ever really committing to anything more. Then, if it didn't work out, at least their relationship wouldn't be too serious.

At least, he hoped it wouldn't be. Considering the way he felt at the moment—all hot and bothered and emotionally invested—there might not be any way to prevent it from becoming serious.

Jocelyn raked her fingers through his hair and kissed him deeply, distracting him from his thoughts. He tried to ease her back onto the sofa, but she rested her hands on his chest. "Remember what I said."

"Precautions?"

"Yes. So why don't we eat that popcorn later? I suspect we're going to work up an appetite."

He smiled down at her and kissed her one more time. "I like the way you think."

She raised a flirty eyebrow and got up, taking him by the hand and leading him to the stairs.

"You know, I was actually surprised that you hired me," Jocelyn said the next morning as she pulled the drapes open across the enormous windows.

Donovan leaned up in bed on one elbow, the white sheet slung across his waist. "Why?"

"Because I'm a woman."

Jocelyn gazed down at his bare, muscular, sun-bronzed chest, and felt her insides melt, but she fought the urge to get back in bed with him and make love again, because they'd already done it twice that morning, and they needed breakfast.

"You came highly recommended," he said. "Not just by Mark. I checked you out online when you left to get your overnight bag."

"Ah, the truth is out." She went to get her bathrobe, on the floor by the door. "But I honestly didn't think you considered me to be a real bodyguard. Part of me thought you just wanted me to come and stay in your penthouse because you thought I was cute and it would be fun."

He looked taken aback. "It *was* fun."

She picked up one of his socks on the floor and flung it at him.

"Seriously," he said, leaning up on one elbow, "I did need a new alarm system."

"But would you have given in so easily to Mark and hired me if I had been a short, bald man?"

He barrowed his eyes at her. "What's with all the questions?"

She pulled on her robe, tied it around her waist, and shrugged.

He pointed at her. "You just want to know if I'm still the player you thought I was when you first met me, and if you're my most recent conquest."

Jocelyn combed her fingers through her hair, wishing he wasn't always so perceptive where her emotions were concerned. Even though she'd come to realize he wasn't at all shallow, she was still afraid of something. She wasn't quite sure what it was yet.

"You can't blame me," she said. "It still boggles my mind that you're single."

His chest heaved with a sigh. "I thought last night you said this was just about enjoying each other while we're here. Are you changing your mind about that?"

He was right, she *had* said they would just enjoy each other. She'd offered him a few nights of pleasure, nothing more.

Was she changing her mind? The thought unnerved her. Everything had been so wonderful last night down at the lake, and through the night in his bed. Donovan had not only given her more pleasure than she'd ever dreamed possible, he'd been caring and loving.

It was all so new. So overwhelming. She didn't know what to make of it.

"Hey, I'm sorry," she said, trying to hide her sudden anxieties. "I shouldn't have brought it up."

"Brought what up, exactly?"

He was staring at her intently. Watching her. Wanting to know what she was getting at.

Was she scaring him off?

"The fact that you hired me," she replied, skirting the *real* question, for him as well as for herself. She needed time to sort out her feelings. "Some people don't trust a woman to do the job. Come on, let's go get some breakfast."

He tossed the sheet off and got out of bed, then fished through his suitcase for a pair of shorts. He pulled them on and followed her down the stairs.

"I hired you because I trusted you," he said. "You have

a competent air about you. I recognized that right away."

Jocelyn entered the kitchen. "Thanks. Why don't I cook breakfast this morning?"

"All right." He sat down on one of the stools at the counter, while she pulled eggs and bacon out of the fridge and set to work. She laid the bacon slices in a skillet to fry.

"So tell me," he said, "why did you leave the Secret Service?"

"To be honest, for the money." She cracked some eggs into a bowl and began to beat them with a whisk.

"That's surprising. I thought you hated that kind of thing."

"I hate people attaching more value to their cars and boats than to their loved ones. I don't hate money. In fact, I appreciate it very much when I can put it to good use. I'm sending my younger sister to Juliard."

He perked up at that. "You never mentioned that before."

"It never came up."

"Do you have any other brothers or sisters?"

"No, just Marie. She's eighteen and a very talented cello player. She moved in with my aunt after my mom died and no one could afford to send her to a good music school, so I went out on my own to try and cover the expense. Besides that, I like the independence of running my own business."

"Are you musical, too?"

She smiled and poured the eggs into the frying pan she'd set on the stove. "I like to sing."

"You are full of surprises. Sing something."

"Not while I'm cooking! I need to concentrate."

"Oh, yeah, I forgot. Cooking is one of the things you *don't* do. But it looks to me like you're doing it pretty well."

She gave him a look over her shoulder. "I didn't say I *couldn't* do it. I just said I didn't like to."

He rose from the stool to come around the counter and approach her from behind. "It seems to me, you're good at everything. This especially…"

He slid his hands around her waist and nibbled her neck, while she stirred the eggs on the stove. Goose bumps erupted and tickled all over her body.

"You're distracting me. I'm going to burn the eggs."

Desire coursed through her. Incapable of resisting his overtures, she set down her spatula and turned around to kiss him. She wrapped her arms around his neck and delighted in the flavor of his mouth. How was it possible a man could push all her buttons with such unbelievable intensity?

After a moment or two, the bacon snapped and sizzled in the skillet, reminding her that she was in charge of breakfast. She smiled and pushed Donovan away. "We can't do this constantly. We're human. We need to eat."

He kissed her on the cheek and returned to the stool. "Being a doctor, you'd think I'd know that."

While Jocelyn cooked breakfast, they talked more about her sister, Marie, then about Donovan's plans with the grief counseling center.

They sat down to eat, discussing what would happen after the police caught Cohen, and how involved Donovan would be in the legal proceedings.

After breakfast, Donovan rose from the table and picked up both their plates. Jocelyn made a move to rise.

"No, you stay and enjoy your coffee," he said. "I'll get this."

He's a dream, she thought, thanking him with a kiss.

A moment later, still in her bathrobe, she rose from the table, pushed the sliding door open, and stepped out onto the deck to enjoy the view of the lake. She sat down on a lounge chair and sipped her coffee, remembering how incredible Donovan had been in bed the night before, how he had brought her to tears when she'd climaxed. They were tears of joy. Tears of hope.

Heaven help her, she was losing control. He may be a dream, she told herself, but he's still your client. A client who has never had, with any woman, a relationship that lasted beyond a few months.

She shifted uneasily in her chair. What was she doing? She was a professional, and she'd broken the cardinal rule: Never get emotionally involved with a client.

Yet here she was, happier than she'd ever been in her life, wanting to touch Donovan and feel his arms around her, wanting to talk to him and fill whatever void still existed in his heart from losing his parents. She wanted to help him find true happiness and show him how wonderful a lasting love could be....

Her mind suddenly clouded with self-doubt. Lasting love? What did she even know of that? She'd been single for years since Tom left her. She still carried around anger at her father for leaving her mother. What did she know of the kind of happiness that came with lifelong love and total trust? Nothing.

A fine pair they made.

Jocelyn heard the sound of pots clanging in the kitchen, and took another sip of her coffee.

Yes, she cared deeply for Donovan. Maybe she was even falling in love with him, but was she brave enough to throw all caution to the wind, and jump in headfirst?

She wasn't sure.

All she knew was that for now, she had to keep her feet on the ground and remember that she was here to do a job, not just enjoy the pleasure he offered.

And at the end of the day, she wasn't entirely confident she had what it might take to lead Donovan out of the lonely place he'd known all his life, and he most likely didn't have what it took to keep a relationship going—even though it was no fault of his own.

Together, they were probably ill-fated. She would do well to remember that, too.

CHAPTER

Eleven

Over the next three days, when they weren't making love in a locked bedroom, Jocelyn and Donovan went fishing, swimming and hiking in the woods. The owner of the cabin delivered live lobsters one night, which Donovan cooked for supper with melted butter and Italian bread. The other evenings, Donovan barbecued, and afterward, they went skinny-dipping in the moonlight.

It was the most romantic few days Jocelyn had ever known in her life—and the most confusing, because everything was so perfect. Donovan was affectionate, attentive and a generous lover. He cooked for her, rubbed her shoulders and listened to whatever she wanted to talk about.

She couldn't imagine that life could be like that every day—that this wasn't some special dream world. There had to be a hitch. There always was.

"Tell me something," Donovan said in bed one night, after they'd made love. "When you were trying to convince me not to buy that black dress for you, you said you could guarantee it was something you'd never wear again. Why? And why do you always wear that plain brown suit and flat shoes, when you'd look terrific in something…else?"

Jocelyn sat up and smiled. "That's a tactful way of telling me I dress like crap."

He laughed. "You know that's not what I meant. You just seem to want to play *down* your looks."

Jocelyn lay back down, resting her cheek on Donovan's shoulder. "I guess I've never been able to stop fighting what I always had to fight as a kid."

"What was that?"

"My father's weird sense of what was important. He wasn't the warmest individual on the planet, and the only time I ever got a smile or a compliment out of him was when I was dressed up like a little princess. He couldn't stand to see me in tattered, dirty play clothes, and he was completely unattracted to my mother when she was wearing her terry cloth bathrobe around the house. Then, when he left, he told her it was because she didn't care enough about her appearance. He took off with a younger woman who wore short skirts, big dangly earrings and lots of hairspray. I'll never forget what she looked like, and my poor mother, who was the kindest, most loving person in the world, never got over that. She became insecure and self-conscious, even when I tried to tell her every day that she was the most beautiful woman in the world to me. I guess I just don't ever want people to like me because I *look* good. I can't stand that kind of superficiality."

Jocelyn couldn't believe she had just told Donovan all of that. She'd never told anyone those things, except her assistant, Tess, and that had been after two years of working together.

He rubbed a thumb over her shoulder. "It doesn't matter what you wear, Jocelyn, you *always* look good."

She kissed his bare chest. "But you're not shallow. Lots of people are, and I don't want or need to dress up to impress *them*."

"But by trying to look like one thing—a tough, untouchable bodyguard—you're doing the same thing your father was doing, only the opposite way. You're still putting a lot of emphasis on your appearance, trying to give off a certain impression, when it doesn't matter. You can wear short skirts if you want to, and you'll still be the same person. You'll still be smart and funny and tough."

She sighed. "That's an interesting way to look at it."

"Maybe. I just wonder if the real reason you've always played down your looks was to keep people away, because you said yourself that you don't believe in happily ever after." He kissed her forehead, and brushed her hair from her eyes. "Jocelyn, I don't want to be one of those people you try to push away."

She leaned up on one elbow to look him in the eye, and spoke with a hint of humor. "You're trying to fix me, aren't you?"

His expression was open and friendly. "I just want you to know that you could wear *anything* in front of me—fancy or plain—and you'd still be extraordinary and gorgeous. And I'm sorry that your father couldn't love you for the person you were on the inside. He was wrong to take his family for granted. He had no idea how lucky he was to have you both. Maybe someday he'll realize that—that family everything."

She rested her head on his chest again. "How did you

get to be so insightful? And so optimistic when you lost everything?"

He thought about that for a moment. "I don't know, maybe it's because of the things I remember about my parents. My grandmother told me they cherished each other, and when they had me, they grew even closer. We were a tight unit, the three of us, and nothing was more important to them than our little family—not their jobs, not their money, not their belongings. Gram told me they were soul mates."

"That's beautiful. You were lucky to grow up with those kinds of ideals."

"Ideals." He gazed down at her. "You don't think it's realistic?"

She shook her head defensively. "I don't mean that. All I know is what I've seen in my life. Maybe the kind of happiness your parents knew is possible for some people."

"But not you?"

She looked at his face, contemplating what she believed. What she thought was possible. Until now, she'd been a skeptic, but Donovan was touching something in her.

She was dreaming of happiness now, imagining a beautiful future with him even though she was scared to death that she was setting herself up for disappointment later on.

Still, she'd never been inclined to dream of a perfect future before, and that said something. Donovan had given her hope.

"I...I guess I would like to believe that maybe it's possible."

His expression warmed at her words. "You're

beautiful." He gathered her into his arms and pressed his mouth hotly to hers.

Jocelyn let all her worries go, and gave herself over completely to the pleasure of his lovemaking, which tonight was like a beautiful, erotic dream.

She would worry about reality tomorrow.

~⊘

"Want to go upstairs and play Monopoly?" Donovan asked, after supper when it looked like rain.

Jocelyn smiled at him. "Monopoly…is that some fancy term for the horizontal mambo?"

He laughed. "No, I think the fancy term for 'the horizontal mambo' is 'the horizontal mambo.' I mean play real Monopoly."

"Why upstairs?" she asked suspiciously.

"I thought we could play it on the bed, in the nude."

Oh, he was fun. She sauntered up close to him and slid a hand down his pants. "It's only fair to warn you, I used to be addicted to Monopoly when I was a kid. You don't know what you're getting into."

He took a deep breath but didn't let it out. "I think you're the one who's getting into something dangerous at the moment. If you're not careful, we'll never even get the game box open."

Jocelyn slowly removed her hand from Donovan's jeans, and backed away toward the stairs. "And which game would that be?"

She started to run, and Donovan chased her.

They bounded up the stairs, laughing and hooting. Donovan caught up just as she neared the bed. He leaped on top of her and flipped her over onto the soft mattress, coming down, kissing her mouth and pressing his pelvis into hers.

"Let's play Monopoly later," Jocelyn whispered, her body tingling with sweet, lusty ideas.

They both rose up on their knees on the bed to take off their T-shirts, still kissing whenever possible. Within seconds, they were out of their jeans and falling back onto the bed.

"Wait!" Jocelyn said. "We didn't lock the door."

"I'll get it." Donovan scrambled off the bed. He flicked the lock and turned on the monitor, then returned to where she lay, naked on top of the covers.

Completely overwhelmed by the loving expression on her face, he stopped at the foot of the bed to gaze down at her, then rested his open palm on his chest. He spoke softly. "You are so beautiful."

Donovan's heart was aching. He couldn't take his eyes off Jocelyn. She was a tiny piece of heaven, there on the bed, waiting for him, her eyes honest and adoring. How could he ever walk away from this?

He gently came down upon her slender body and held her close in his arms.

He felt joyful, more complete somehow as his lips brushed hers and her body melted perfectly into his. They were made for each other, and he was completely in her power, overcome by the compulsion to hold her tighter and closer, to make love to her tonight and every night until he drew his last breath.

His blood quickened in his veins at the exhilarating decision—that he wanted her forever.

The absolute certainty was strange and foreign, and so

potent that he felt it like an inferno in his chest. He didn't want to ever let her go.

She wrapped her long, lovely legs around him and kissed his neck, ran her hands up and down his spine, and he squeezed her tight against him.

"Jocelyn," he whispered, running his hands through her hair. "I've never felt like this."

She sighed amorously. "I've never felt like this, either, Donovan."

He made love to her in the twilight, slowly. Very slowly, with deliberate attention to what she was feeling, intensifying the things she liked.

She moved with him in harmony on the bed. Sexually, he had come to know her very well these past few days. He knew what stirred her into that whirlwind of excitement, and what sent her soaring.

He took his time delivering the pleasure tonight. He spent each passing heartbeat watching her face and giving her all that he had. She opened her eyes and gazed up at him lazily, then cupped his face in her hands. Time seemed to stand still. Donovan's heart swelled with love.

Yes, it was love.

"Jocelyn." He lowered his body to hers and held her tightly in his arms. "I don't want this to end."

He didn't just mean their lovemaking. He meant all of it.

Then he brought her with him to the edge of desire, then over the edge to the beyond.

It was different this time. The deepest places in his heart were involved and committed.

He held her tightly, squeezing her close, wishing he could get even closer. "Jocelyn…"

For a long while, they lay in each other's arms until the twilight turned to darkness and rain began to tap on the skylight over their heads. Seconds later, it intensified to a torrential downpour, drumming noisily on the glass.

Jocelyn snuggled closer. "I guess we won't be stargazing tonight."

Donovan kissed her forehead. "I like the sound of the rain. It reminds me of camping with my grandmother in her trailer when I was a kid. We always had the worst luck with weather, but it was nice all the same. Cozy."

"My parents took me tenting when I was really little, but only a few times. We weren't much into family vacations. Then when Dad left, we didn't do much other than the usual routine. I'd love to go to a campground someday."

"Let's do it," Donovan said.

"Yeah. Sure."

He tipped her face up to look into her eyes, but he couldn't see her expression in the darkness. "No, I really mean it. Let's go as soon as they catch Cohen. As soon as he's behind bars. We'll bring a bottle of champagne."

She nodded, but he sensed a sadness in her. "What's wrong?" he asked,

"Nothing."

He sat up. "No, something's wrong. You seem down."

"It's nothing, Donovan."

"It is something. Tell me what's the matter."

At last, she sat up, too. "Reality is settling in."

"What do you mean?"

"I mean, we're going to have to leave this place eventually, and I've been having such a good time."

"So have I, but we can have a good time in Chicago, too."

She shrugged. "I just think that when we go back to our

real lives, this will seem like a dream."

He leaned away from her to flick on the light. They both squinted as their eyes adjusted. "Didn't you hear what I said before? That I didn't want this to end?"

"I thought you were talking about—" she waved her hand over the bed "—this."

He shook his head. "No, I was talking about *all* of it. I want to keep seeing you, Jocelyn."

She swiveled to put her feet on the floor so that he was looking at her bare back. "I'm not sure that would be a good idea."

His heart wrenched painfully in his chest. *Here we go...* It was time for the inevitable disappearing act.

But no... He was certain she cared for him. He couldn't have mistaken the way she touched him, the way she looked at him and spoke to him. They'd talked about so many things over the past few days. They'd opened up to each other. They'd made love.

"Why not?" he asked. "We're great together, and once you're no longer my bodyguard, there won't be any reason to resist this."

"There's a big reason."

He swallowed hard over a sickening lump of dread in his gut. "Is there something you haven't told me?"

She turned slightly on the bed to look at him. "No, it's nothing like that. It's what I've told you before—that I have a hard time believing in happily ever after."

She must have seen the expression of shock and hurt on his face, because she reached for his hand. "It's not that I don't trust you. It's that I don't trust myself not to fall so hard for you that I would never be able to recover if it ended."

"What makes you so sure it would end?"

"It always ends."

"That's not true. Lots of people spend their entire lives together."

"Not people like you and me."

Donovan couldn't speak for a moment. He raked a hand through his hair. "Jocelyn, I felt that way, too. Maybe I still do a little. I can't see into the future, and hell, I'm as scared as you are about how this might turn out, but I've never felt this way about anyone before. This is different. So if the circumstances are different, maybe we can be different, too."

She shook her head. "I don't know, Donovan. My parents were in love once, and look what happened to them. My dad left my mom for a younger, prettier woman and never looked back. My mom was devastated, because she really, really loved him. She never got over it. She was still crying years later when she looked at his picture. It was heartbreaking for me to see, and I don't want to go through that. I don't want to be like her someday."

"So you're going to pass up on what we have together, because there's a *chance* it might not work out? Jocelyn, you might be missing out on something really great."

"But I'm not a risk taker. I do what it takes to prevent dangerous things from happening."

"That's a fine philosophy for your work," he said, "but not for your life. If you don't risk the bad, you'll never experience the really great stuff. I've been alone my whole life, and you're the first person I've ever felt close to. I can't let you disappear. I need you."

She turned her back on him again. "You're just feeling this way because of the situation. You feel vulnerable, and I make you feel safe. What you feel isn't permanent. When Cohen is caught, you won't need me."

"I *will* need you," he replied, "and it has nothing to do with Cohen. Don't you trust me? Don't you believe that I care for you, and that I want you? Hell, Jocelyn, I'm in love with you."

She turned to look at him, her face pale with astonishment. She sat motionless, staring at him.

"I love you," he firmly repeated, sliding closer and pushing a lock of hair away from her face. "I've never said that to anyone before. Doesn't that count for something?"

"Tom said those words to me, too, and my father said them to my mother."

"I'm not Tom or your father. I'm Donovan Knight, the man who loves you and wants to spend his life with you."

Jocelyn got off the bed, as if it had caught fire. "What are you saying?"

"I'm saying I want to marry you. If you want to marry *me*."

Her eyes grew wide like saucers. She grabbed her head in her hands and paced to the door. "This is too fast! You're not being sensible. We hardly know each other."

He tried to follow her. "That's not true. We know each other better than some people can know each other in a lifetime. We click."

Her face winced. She looked like she was going to cry. "Please don't do this, Donovan."

"Why not?"

"Because I want to keep us both safe, at least until I can feel more sure of things."

"Love is not a security assignment, Jocelyn. There will never be guarantees."

"That's what scares me."

He let out a frustrated breath. "But if it works out…"

"*If* it works out? I can't hang my hopes or my future happiness on anything that begins with the word *if.*" She reached for her clothes and pulled her T-shirt over her head. "I'm sorry, Donovan, I need to be alone for a while. I'll be in my room."

With that, she walked out and left him reeling with shock and dismay.

What just happened? Jocelyn wondered frantically as she shut her bedroom door and leaned against it. How had a simple week in this cabin, protecting a client, gotten so out of control? And who started the heavy ball rolling? Had she encouraged Donovan subconsciously somehow? Maybe she had been dreaming a little too much about happily ever after, and she'd communicated that to him.

Or was he right? Did they click like they'd never clicked with anyone else? Was this a once-in-a-lifetime fairy tale?

Jocelyn dropped her forehead into the heels of her hands and padded to the bed. If only she had more experience with this sort of thing. She'd shied away from dating ever since Tom cheated on her, and she was way out of her league here. For all she knew, maybe all infatuations felt like this at first—a burning fire that refused to be extinguished. Maybe it was just lust. Maybe it would pass for both of them as soon as they got home.

Or maybe it wouldn't.

She lay down on the bed she hadn't slept on since they'd arrived. What was she going to do?

Her cell phone rang in the kitchen, and she jumped. Jocelyn hurried out of her room to answer it. "Hello?"

"Jocelyn, it's Tess. How's everything going?"

Jocelyn contemplated how she should answer that question. "Oh, you know, everything's fine."

"Yeah? Have you been having a nice time?"

Jocelyn recognized Tess's playful tone, but she wasn't in the mood for innuendo, nor was she willing to divulge details about her personal life when she didn't even understand those details herself. Tess probably wouldn't even believe it if she told her. *Yes, I've been having a wonderful time, and Prince Charming just proposed marriage....*

"What's up?" Jocelyn asked.

Thankfully, Tess stuck to business. "I have news. The police picked up Ben Cohen this afternoon. He's in custody and he confessed to everything."

"You're kidding me." Jocelyn sank onto a chair at the table. "That didn't take long."

"Yeah, it's great, isn't it? You can come home anytime. Oh, and I tentatively booked you on a new assignment. A high profile environmental activist has been getting threatening letters."

Feeling numb all of a sudden, Jocelyn watched the rain slide down the windows in fast-moving rivulets. It was over. They'd caught Cohen. It was time to go home.

"Jocelyn? Are you there?"

She snapped herself back to reality. "Yes, Tess, I'm here. That's great. Um...we'll pack up and leave tonight. I'm sure the police will want to speak to Donovan first thing in the morning."

"Yes, they did ask about that." There was a long silence on the other end of the line. "So what do you want me to do about the environmental activist? Do you want to take that assignment? She's pretty anxious."

Jocelyn continued to stare at the rain-covered window. Lightning flashed somewhere in the distance.

Her heart throbbed a few times in her chest, then she took a deep breath and stood up.

"Yes. I'll take it, and tell her I'll start immediately. I can do the advance work tomorrow."

She ended the call and turned around. Donovan was standing at the bottom of the stairs, staring at her, his eyebrows drawn together with concern.

Jocelyn's stomach flared with nervous knots. "I didn't realize you were listening."

His voice was low and controlled. "That's obvious." He slowly strode toward her. "What's going on? And why do I get the feeling that if you have it your way, after tonight I'm never going to see you again?"

Jocelyn strode to her room to start packing her things. "It won't be like that. We've gotten close, Donovan. We'll keep in touch."

He followed her and stood in the doorway. "The old 'we'll still be friends' routine? Come on, Jocelyn," he said bitterly.

She opened dresser drawers and pulled out her clothes, balling them up and tossing them into her suitcase.

Donovan strode to her and took hold of her arm. "Stop packing for a second and talk to me."

"We can talk in the car," she replied. "I want to get going because it's a long drive, and I want to get you back to your penthouse by midnight."

"So you're just going to drop me off and keep going?"

She paused a moment to face him squarely. "There's no more danger. Cohen is behind bars, and there's no point in you being charged my fees for another day. Today ends at midnight."

"Oh, so you're doing me a favor, is that it? Saving me a

few bucks? And if I asked you to stay the night, I'd have to *pay* for that, would I?"

Jocelyn's lips parted. She supposed she deserved that, for all the pain she was inflicting upon him. All because she was afraid to take a risk with him.

Feeling defeated, she sat down on the edge of the bed. "Donovan, I'm sorry about this. I know I'm being a jerk."

He stood a few feet away, listening. She gazed up at him imploringly. "Maybe we could see each other, but take it slow. Cool our jets a little and try to be casual about this."

He considered that for a moment, then shook his head, his expression grim. "No, I don't think I can do that. I'm in love with you, Jocelyn. Passionately. I don't want 'casual.' I want to come home to you every night and wake up with you every morning. Life's too short to do it any other way."

Jocelyn sighed heavily and stared down at the white T-shirt she was squeezing into a ball on her lap. "I'm not sure I can be that person, Donovan. I would always be holding back, waiting for the other shoe to drop, and you deserve better. You *need* something better, because you've never had it, and I can see how much you want it. Believing that I'm the one for you…it's just wishful thinking. You're in love with the person I was here, but this isn't the real me, and frankly, it's not the real you, either. We were just pretending. Living a fantasy. Pretending that life was perfect and nothing could touch us. It won't be like that when we go back."

He stared at her in the lamplight, then he nodded and began to back away. "All right. I'll go pack my things."

He left the room. Jocelyn was shocked. Shocked by everything she had just said, and shocked that he was gone without a fight.

She continued to sit on the bed, staring after him in silence. Her eyes filled with hot, stinging tears. Her insides were churning.

She hated hurting him like this. But wasn't it better to do it now, when it was just an infatuation, before things got truly serious?

A tear trickled down her cheek and she wiped it away.

When was the last time she'd cried? She couldn't remember. She'd spent her whole life working so hard to be tough, pushing pain and vulnerability away. She'd never cried when Tom left her. Anger and resentment had smothered any possibility of tears.

Looking back on it, she supposed she had never truly felt that Tom's heart was involved—or her father's, either. They'd been callous men, more concerned with appearances and what the neighbors might think than what she or anyone else was feeling.

Donovan was the opposite. He felt everything deeply, which was why he was working on a grief counseling center for kids, because his heart was still enduring the hole left behind when his parents drove over that cliff and perished in front of his eyes. It was why he was still single. He was not cavalier about love.

Yet she had been savage toward his wounded heart. What did that make her? How could she have done that? Was she really the cold, tough, unfeeling person she made herself out to be? In not wanting to be like her mother, had she become like her father?

Her chest throbbed with agony. She didn't feel like her

father on the inside. She felt more like a wounded bird, who couldn't manage to find her wings.

Yet she had found them briefly these past few days with Donovan, when she'd clutched at him and cried out his name in the darkness, or when she'd laughed with him or told him secrets about her childhood.

Was it too late for her to find her wings? Too late to believe in a love that could last forever?

She gazed up at the ceiling and heard Donovan slamming things around upstairs. She didn't know. She just didn't know.

After a long, silent drive back to Chicago in the pouring rain and darkness, Jocelyn escorted Donovan up to his penthouse. She did a thorough search to make sure everything was okay, then stood in his marble vestibule, preparing to say goodbye. It was shortly before midnight.

"So this is it," Donovan said flatly.

She flinched at his icy tone. "Donovan, I'm sorry. I've accepted another assignment for tomorrow and—"

"You don't have to explain. You already did that at the cabin."

They stared at each other for a few seconds, then Donovan stuck out his hand. "It was a pleasure working with you. If you need references, I'd be happy to provide them. You did an excellent job with the security."

Feeling numb and confused, Jocelyn gazed up at his handsome face, listened to his detached tone, and shook his hand. "Please, Donovan…"

She didn't know what to say. She wasn't any good at this.

She'd never been in this situation before, and she'd spent half her life fighting to keep people at a distance. He was doing the same thing to her now, and it was killing her inside.

Rising up on her toes, she leaned toward him and kissed him on the cheek. "I had a great time with you. I won't forget it."

"Neither will I." His voice told her he was shaken by the kiss. So was she.

"I should go. It's late and we both need to catch up on some sleep."

Donovan nodded.

She walked to the elevator and pressed the down button. With her back to him, she listened for his door closing, but it didn't. He was still standing there, watching her. Her stomach tightened into knots. Her heart was racing.

Something was tugging at her, telling her to turn around and dash back into his arms, kiss him and tell him how sorry she was. Tell him that she loved him and she never wanted to let him go.

But her brain wouldn't let her. What about tomorrow, she heard herself asking, and the day after that? She couldn't make important decisions like this on a heart-splitting impulse. She had to think about the ramifications of her actions. She needed time….

The elevator dinged and the brass doors opened smoothly. She stepped inside.

She didn't want to turn around. She couldn't look at his face one more time, because she might change her mind. Yet she had to turn around to press the lobby button.

Jocelyn took a deep breath and faced the front. Whatever she was afraid of was a nonissue. Donovan's door was just clicking shut.

"I can't believe you got on that elevator," Tess said from her desk, tearing the paper off the bottom of her blueberry muffin. "Prince Charming wants to marry you, and you walk away."

Back in the familiar feel of her brown pantsuit, Jocelyn stood at the filing cabinet in the reception area of her office, looking for something in the top drawer. "Life isn't a fairy tale. It all happened too fast. People can't make important decisions like that based on a few romantic days with their bodyguard at a lakeside retreat, when their life's in danger."

"*He* did."

She threw Tess an impatient glare. "That doesn't make it sensible. He would have regretted it. I did him a favor last night. He'll realize that as soon as he gets back into his regular routine. I give each of us three days tops to forget about this. Where's the file on limo services?"

"How can you be so sure?" Tess asked. "And what about *you*? Did you do *yourself* a favor last night, turning down a marriage proposal to the most handsome man alive, who also happens to be a rich doctor and great in bed?"

Jocelyn held up a hand. "Please don't go there. It just feels like a pipe dream, and I don't want to think about that."

"Why not? If you don't think about it, you're not facing it, and you'll be living in a bubble, out of touch with reality."

"Tess, I don't want to—"

The phone rang. Tess picked it up. "Mackenzie Security."

Her eyes lifted and she started pointing frantically at the phone, mouthing the words, *It's him!*

There could have been a power surge in Jocelyn's veins. She stood at the filing cabinet, panic filling every corner of her being, while she watched Tess, and waited for her to say something.

Tess kept her gaze lowered. She was nodding and saying, "Certainly," in that professional tone she had down pat.

A few seconds later, she hung up the phone and Jocelyn's heart broke into a thousand pieces.

"What did he want?"

Tess grimaced. "He wants me to e-mail him the bill instead of using regular mail, so that he can drop his check off today."

A lump the size of a grapefruit was forming in Jocelyn's throat. She couldn't speak.

"Maybe he wants to see you," Tess offered helpfully.

Jocelyn knew better. She shook her head and went back to what she was doing. Her fingers crawled over the tops of her files. "I don't think so. He wants to put a tidy finish on things."

"Maybe not. Maybe he'll show up with flowers."

Jaded as she was, Jocelyn sighed and shook her head again, fighting off the tiny fragment of hope that—despite her attempts to crush it—still lived inside her.

That tenacious little hope languished, however, later in the day, when a check arrived by courier.

~*⌐*

Jocelyn had given herself three days to get over Donovan.

Three weeks had gone by.

After finishing her assignment with the environmental activist, she sat in her apartment eating Cheerios and watching television at ten o'clock at night. She had no work lined up for the next day. She'd told Tess to give her some time off. She'd never needed time off before, but she'd never felt tired before, either.

Tired. That was an understatement. All she wanted to do was crawl into bed and lie there for a week. Everything had gotten so...busy. There was nothing to smile about. The environmental activist treated her like she was invisible—which was nothing new. She expected and even encouraged that from her principals. But since her week with Donovan, she'd come to realize that being invisible wasn't all it was cracked up to be. Sure it was okay on the job, but what about outside of work? Who was she? Who actually cared about her?

With Donovan, she had felt appreciated and alive. She'd felt like a woman. Someone with an identity, even though she was away from everything that was a part of who she was—her apartment, her car, her office. Donovan had made her feel like she mattered in the world, even when she was naked, swimming in the lake.

What she'd had with him was the least materialistic thing she'd ever known. Yet it was the most real. And like an idiot, she had walked away from it. Worse than walked away. She had hurt him in the process, when he'd been hurt far too much in his life.

Would he ever forgive her? she wondered, longing for the bliss and tranquility she'd felt in his arms day after day when she had been in his employ. She had thought it would fade away by now, but the hurt was only getting worse. She missed him. *Oh God*, how she missed him. What a coward she had been.

She rose from the sofa to put her empty bowl in the dishwasher, then poured soap in and pressed the start button. She went to her bedroom and gazed at her empty bed, then at her treadmill and free weights, thought about what she did for a living, all the dangerous situations she'd been in. Wasn't she supposed to be tough and strong? What happened to her? Where was her grit?

A vision of Donovan's handsome face appeared in her mind, along with the memory of his kiss and his tenderness. Three weeks had gone by and she was nowhere near to being over him.

This was not just a fleeting infatuation.

A new sense of purpose filled her. She went to her closet and began rifling through her clothes, looking for something feminine to wear. She'd had three weeks to think about Donovan, and in her heart and soul she finally knew that this was not an impulse.

Tomorrow, she was going to see Donovan again, and come hell or high water, she would rise above her fears. For the first time in her life, she was going to take a risk with her personal life.

How it would turn out, she had no idea. She would just have to have faith, and leap.

Jocelyn was getting out of the shower when her cell phone rang in her bedroom. Wearing a towel, she padded down the hall to answer it. "Hello?"

"Hi, it's Tess. Something's happened and I thought you should know about it."

Recognizing the sober tone in Tess's voice, Jocelyn sat down on the edge of her bed. "What is it?"

"Ben Cohen was released yesterday. Apparently, there was mix-up with the warrant they used to search his apartment. A couple of officers crossed wires and they each thought the other had the warrant, and they ended up using one that was meant for someone else."

"Oh, no."

"You might want to go and see Dr. Knight. Do you want me to call his penthouse?"

"Yes, and try his cell phone, too. Tell him to lock the door and not to go out, and that I'm on my way."

Jocelyn threw off the towel and got dressed. Fifteen minutes later, she was in her car on her way to his place, when her phone rang again. "Yes?"

"It's Tess. I've been trying his penthouse and his cell phone, but everything's going to voice mail. I called the hospital but he's not working today. I haven't been able to get in touch with him, Jo. I hope everything's okay."

A cold chill ran down Jocelyn's spine. "Keep trying. Maybe he's out on the terrace or in the shower or something. I'm near his place now. I'll call you when I know something."

She parked, holstered her gun, and dashed into the lobby.

"Briggs, is Dr. Knight at home?" she asked the security guard.

"No, Ms. Mackenzie. He's gone out for a run. He left about half an hour ago."

"Thanks." She pushed through the revolving door and called Tess again. "He's gone for a run. I'm going to look for him, but keep trying his penthouse and cell in case we don't cross paths. Tell him to lock his door and not to move until I get there, and call me if you reach him."

Jocelyn ended the call and slipped her phone into her pocket. She started running down the street toward the park which had been his regular route before he'd hired her. She was glad she'd worn her sneakers.

The sun warmed her head and shoulders. She worked up a sweat, running in her jeans and blazer, but all she cared about was finding Donovan.

She reached the park and shaded her eyes. She scanned the crowds of people on rollerblades and walking their dogs. There were lots of runners on the paths, but no sign of Donovan.

Then she spotted someone in running gear, sitting on the ground a distance away, leaning against a tree in the shade, fiddling with a sprig of grass.

It was Donovan. A cry of relief spilled from her lips. *Thank God.*

She perused the surroundings, looking for any suspicious-looking characters, and approached.

His gaze shot up. His face paled when she came to a halt before him. "Jocelyn, what are you doing here?"

She had to work hard to catch her breath. She wiped her forehead with the back of her hand. "I'm so glad I found you."

He frowned. "Why?"

"Something's happened. Ben Cohen was released on a technicality yesterday. You're not safe."

He said nothing for a few seconds. "I see."

"I need to escort you back to your building."

Donovan stared up at Jocelyn's dark eyes and full lips, her cheeks flushed from the exertion of running through the park in jeans and a blazer, and wondered how it was possible that he could still be so completely in love with her after the way they'd parted three weeks ago.

Between now and then, he'd flip-flopped between feeling furious with her one minute, to picking up the phone and dialing her number to ask her out the next—only to hang up before it rang. He hadn't been able to think of anything but her.

Now, he was disappointed. He'd thought she had come here for personal reasons—that she would pour out her heart, tell him how much she missed him, and that he'd finally be able to take her into his arms. But she was only here because of his stalker. He'd made the wrong assumption, like he'd been wrong about everything else where she was concerned.

Rising to his feet, he tried not to look directly into her eyes. If he was ever going to feel normal again, he would have to forget about her and convince himself that she' was right. That what they'd experienced at the lake hadn't been real.

This was the real Jocelyn. All business. No heart. No vulnerability.

"That's fine," he coolly said. "I'll go with you for now, but I think—because we were personally involved—that it would be best if I hired someone else for protection. You understand, I hope."

If he was going to protect himself from falling under her spell again, he couldn't even consider inviting her back into his life.

Her lips parted. With surprise? Or was it something else? If it was angst or sorrow, it could be no worse than what he'd suffered when she'd insisted on ending things between them. He couldn't let himself feel guilty about that.

"All right, let's go this way." She recovered quickly from whatever she'd been feeling. Always the professional, he thought bitterly.

Keeping her eyes on the path and the people approaching them from any side, Jocelyn walked beside Donovan. They didn't talk. He knew she was focused on what she was doing, and he, to be frank, couldn't have made his mouth work if he tried. He just wanted this to be over with.

They approached his building and waited to cross the street. All of a sudden, from out of nowhere, a gunshot fired past Donovan's head and chiseled a piece of brick out of the building behind them.

Jocelyn immediately shielded him with her body and forced him to the ground behind a parked car, just like she'd done the last time. People on the street were screaming and running. His heart hammered in his chest.

Another shot blasted by and missed.

"He's not giving up!" Jocelyn drew her gun and looked around for where the shots were coming from.

Donovan looked up. "He's there!"

"Where?"

Donovan pointed. "Around the side of my building. He's aiming his gun at us."

Jocelyn peered out, just as a bullet hit a nearby telephone pole. Wood splintered next to them. Seizing an opportunity, she fired at Cohen and miraculously knocked his gun out of his hand. Donovan heard Cohen groan with pain, then saw him bolt.

"He's running!" Donovan sprinted out into the street to go after him.

"Donovan, wait!" Jocelyn followed.

Sirens began to wail from somewhere in the distance, but Donovan wasn't stopping. He had the chance to catch Cohen now, and he couldn't wait for the cops.

He chased Cohen down the alley, leaping over garbage cans, and followed him across a back street. Jocelyn's footfalls tapped the ground not far behind him. He knew she had her gun, and Cohen was unarmed. He wasn't giving up now.

He was gaining on Cohen. The guy was no runner.

A minute later, Donovan hurled himself through the air and tackled Cohen from behind, into a pile of wooden crates in another alley. He felt his arm scrape against something. His jaw cracked against the back of Cohen's head, and he tasted blood in his mouth.

Cohen scrambled beneath him to get away, but the sound of a gun cocking next to his head made him freeze.

"Hold it right there," Jocelyn said, her legs braced apart. "Move one muscle and you'll be leaving here in a body bag."

Donovan took one look at her—tough as nails—and rolled off Cohen, who raised his hands in the air.

Just then, a cop car skidded to a halt on the street at the

end of the alley and a swarm of uniformed officers came bounding around the corner. Still sitting on the pavement, Donovan wiped his bloody lip with the back of his hand.

"Hey, Ms. Mackenzie," one of the cops said, just before he grabbed Cohen and cuffed him. "Nice work."

She lowered her weapon. "It was Dr. Knight who did most of it, Charlie. He tackled him like a linebacker."

Her shoulders rose and fell with a deep intake of breath as she looked down at Donovan. "Are you all right?" She offered her hand to pull him to his feet.

He inspected the blood on his hand. "I'll live."

She gazed up at him, then something in her face changed. The tough-as-nails persona fell away, and a softness took its place—along with a few tears spilling down her cheeks.

Donovan was breathing hard. So was she, as she took three swift strides toward him and threw her arms around his neck.

The whole world disappeared around them. Donovan didn't care what was happening to Cohen. He was barely aware of the cops reading the guy his rights. All that mattered was Jocelyn, there in his arms, trembling with tears and weeping onto his shoulder.

"It's over," he said, stroking her hair. "He's in custody now."

She shook her head and sniffled. "That's not why I'm crying. I do this stuff all the time."

He couldn't help laughing. "Then why *are* you crying?"

She looked up at him. Her face was wet and her nose was running. "Because I was afraid I was going to lose you, and I'd never get the chance to tell you how sorry I am."

The officer named Charlie appeared beside them. *Great timing.*

"I'm going to need statements from the both of you."

Donovan and Jocelyn stepped apart. Jocelyn wiped under her nose and quickly collected herself, then began to explain what happened, as well as the fact that Cohen's gun had flown out of his hand back at Donovan's building and needed to be picked up. The officer had some questions for Donovan, too, then when they were done, he closed his notebook and said he'd be in touch.

Donovan and Jocelyn stood in the alley, alone at last. Neither of them said anything for a moment or two.

"Are you okay?" Donovan asked, wishing they hadn't been interrupted before. Jocelyn had been in his arms, and he wanted her back. He wanted to understand what she was sorry for, exactly.

It wasn't going to happen now, however. The moment had passed, and he wasn't sure what was going on anymore. She was staring at the ground, looking like a tough E.P.P. again.

"Do you want to go back to my place for a drink?" he asked, not sure where this might lead—he was still afraid to hope. "You're off duty now, and I sure as hell could use a double shot of whisky. I've never apprehended a stalker before." He held up his hand and showed her that it was still shaking.

He managed to get a smile out of her at least. "I'd love a beer," she said.

Elation moved through him.

The very next second, his gut twisted into knots as he smiled down at her and comprehended how much of his future happiness depended on the next half hour of his life. He wasn't entirely quite sure what to expect.

D onovan pulled his key from his shoe wallet and unlocked the door to his penthouse.

"Wait." Jocelyn touched his arm and held him back. "Let me go in first and check things out. You never know."

Donovan exhaled heavily. She was dedicated to her work, and he respected her for it, even when it got in the way of his goal to make this drink personal rather than professional.

He waited by the door while she disarmed the alarm system and checked his penthouse for God knew what. A short time later, she came sauntering out of his bedroom.

What he wouldn't give to see her sauntering out of there every morning for the rest of his life....

Brushing those hopes aside, he smiled. "Everything okay?"

"It looks fine. Now...how about that beer?"

"Coming right up." He gestured toward the sofa with his hand. "Make yourself comfortable."

It felt strange, treating her like a guest when she'd been his roommate not that long ago.

Donovan went to change into a pair of jeans and a clean shirt, then went to the kitchen and pulled two cold ones out of the fridge and twisted off the caps. He carried them down the hall.

He stopped in his tracks, however, when he heard his Eric Clapton CD playing. Memories of those early nights with Jocelyn came flooding back. He remembered discovering, for the first time, something of the real woman beneath the suit and the tough girl image. He remembered the way she had smiled when she'd heard these songs.

He swallowed hard over his unease, his fear that today might end the same as that pivotal night at the cabin—when an argument and a breakup had wedged them apart.

"Here you go." He entered the living room and handed her the bottle of beer.

"You decided to forgo the whisky?"

"Yeah. Sometimes a cold brew is what a guy really needs. Cheers. Here's to Cohen behind bars again."

They clinked the spouts of their bottles and took the first few sips.

"Have a seat," Donovan said, feeling awkward and out of his element, trying to be casual when all he really wanted to do was take Jocelyn into his arms and kiss every inch of her.

That would probably scare her off, though—to put it mildly—and at this point, he was more than willing to go slow and cool his jets, like she'd asked him to do, at the cabin.

Damn, he'd stand on his head for a week if it would change her mind about ending their relationship.

She sat down and kicked off her shoes, then tucked her

jean clad legs up under her. "Donovan, I'm glad you invited me here, because I really wanted to talk to you today."

He cleared his throat and sat down beside her. "About Cohen?"

For a moment, she just stared at him. "No. I...I know that's why I went looking for you at the park, but the truth is, I was planning to come and see you before I knew about his release."

Donovan remembered how he'd felt when he first looked up at her in the park, how he'd hoped she was there just for him. Then the disappointment...

He waited in silence for her to continue.

She lowered her gaze, drawing little circles on his upholstery with the tip of her index finger. "I've...missed you."

All his nerve endings began to buzz.

"The past few weeks have been hell," she continued. "I haven't been able to stop thinking about you, and I hate the way things ended between us. That week at the cabin was the best week of my life, and I totally screwed it up."

"You didn't screw it up," he said gently, covering her hand with his.

"Yes, I did." Her voice quavered, but she looked him directly in the eye. "I'm sorry for being such a coward."

He sat there, dumbfounded and bewildered. "What are you saying?"

"I'm saying that I was an idiot. I was afraid to love you because of the things I remember about my father and Tom. I was afraid of getting hurt, but walking away from you hurt even more. I want to go back to what we had. I only hope that you can forgive me for causing you pain, and I hope you still..." She lowered her gaze.

Donovan inched closer to her and cradled her chin in his hand, lifted her face meet his eyes. "You hope I still what?"

Her eyes were wet and bloodshot as she gazed up at him. "I hope you still want me."

His entire being heated from the inside out. Everything was pulsing with excitement and relief. How could she even doubt if for a minute?

"I never stopped wanting you, Jocelyn. I wanted you the first second I saw you, standing at my door with that serious glare in your eyes, just like I want you now."

She blinked up at him, all woman—vulnerable, feminine. Her lips were moist and parted and a pulse of arousal began to throb deep inside his body. He took her face in his hands and covered her mouth with his.

Jocelyn wrapped her arms around his neck, and he pulled her into his arms, deepening the kiss and letting his hands slide down the soft curves of her body. How many nights had he lain awake dreaming of this? How many nights had he wished she would come to him and tell him she wanted to go back to what they were when they were together?

Yet none of those dreams could compare to the flesh and blood feel of this woman in his arms now, her mouth tasting deliciously of beer and her hair smelling of citrus. He couldn't get enough. He didn't think he would ever get enough....

"I love you," he whispered in her ear, nibbling at her lobe and feeling her writhe with rapture and delight. "You're the only woman I've ever wanted."

"I don't know what I did to deserve you."

"You were just you."

He took her mouth again with a passionate intensity, and drank in the luscious flavor of her whole being.

"I promise I won't get spooked this time," she said, tipping her head back as he dropped open kisses upon her neck. "These weeks away from you gave me time to understand that what we had wasn't just an infatuation. I needed time to think about everything, because as you know, I'm not impulsive. But I'm here now, Donovan, and I'm yours. Completely."

He drew back to look her in the eye. "You're sure about that?"

"I've never been more sure of anything."

He kissed her again, long and slow, then sat back. "Will you stay here for a second?"

"Sure." She watched him curiously as he kissed her on the forehead and left the room.

He went to the safe in his bedroom and turned the knob left, twenty-four, then right, sixty-eight, then left again to five and back to zero. He couldn't go fast enough.

Finally, the safe clicked open and he reached inside for the little velvet box he'd been saving his entire life. His heart was pounding like a hammer.

He paused a moment and took a breath, feeling his whole world shift on its axis. Everything was changing. He slipped the box into his pocket.

Donovan walked down the hall and returned to the living room, where Jocelyn waited on the sofa, all smiles, looking flushed and beautiful, like an angel from heaven. He slowly made his way toward her and knelt at her feet.

His heart was racing. He'd never been so nervous about anything in his life.

He took her hands in his and labored to keep his voice

steady and controlled. "You're the one, Jocelyn. I know it as clearly as I know my own name. You're the one I want to spend my life with, the one I want to grow old with, and I promise I will make you happy forever, and I will never, ever leave you, if only you'll say yes."

Her eyes were sparkling. She began to smile. "Yes to what?"

"Yes to marrying me. I didn't propose properly last time. This time, I'm doing it right." He reached into his pocket, withdrew the box and opened it before her. The diamond ring glittered magically. "This was my mother's. She left it to me in her will. My grandmother said it signified everlasting love, and that it would represent my mother's love for me even after she was gone, and that she hoped I would pass it on to my own children. It means a lot to me. Will you wear it, and give it to our child some day?"

Jocelyn covered her mouth with trembling fingers and stared down at the beautiful, sparkling, pear-shaped diamond.

"It's the most beautiful ring I've ever seen." She took it out of the box and tried it on. "And it fits perfectly."

Donovan got up off his knees to sit beside her on the sofa again. He touched her cheek lovingly. "You're meant to wear it, I guess."

She began to nod. "Maybe so. I feel good about this. I feel *really* good about it."

He exhaled a long sigh of contentment, then kissed her again, tenderly and passionately, stroking her hair and her shoulders. "I feel good, too. I'll always feel good with you in my life, Jocelyn. I hope you don't want a long engagement."

She smiled seductively. "I'll marry you tomorrow if you can get the time off."

A swell of arousal moved through him at the sexy, silky tone of her voice.

"Tomorrow might be a little difficult," he said. "How about the day after?"

"What's so important tomorrow?" she asked, laying teasing little kisses on his chin and neck. The feel of her wet lips on his flesh sent a message to his nether regions, and he began to rise to this tantalizing occasion.

"Tomorrow I'm helping you move in here," he replied. "That is, if you *want* to live here."

"Of course I do." Her voice became serious. "It was your parents' place, Donovan, and look what they created while they lived here." She touched her palm to his cheek. "We have a lot to look forward to, don't we? But for now, I only want one thing."

"And what's that?"

Her eyes glimmered with desire. She pulled off her shirt to reveal a red, lace teddy. "I want you to carry me to your bedroom, so I can thank you for bringing out the woman in me."

His hunger for his new fiancée intensified. He rubbed his nose up against hers. "We'll get there faster if we run."

She laughed and leaped off the sofa. "As long as you promise to go slow when we get there."

Desire burned through his body at the idea of making love to Jocelyn slowly, for the rest of the day and long into the night, in the bedroom that would become theirs, forever. "I wouldn't have it any other way."

Dear Reader,

Thank you for taking the time to read PROMISE YOU'LL STAY. I hope you enjoyed it. If you did, you might want to check out the romantic women's fiction novels in my bestselling *Color of Heaven* series. Read on for an extended excerpt from THE COLOR OF FOREVER, which is available now.

If you're a fan of historical romance, I have many books available in that genre, and you can see all the titles and covers on my website at www.juliannemaclean.com. While you're there, be sure to visit my giveaway page where I send an autographed print edition to one lucky newsletter subscriber each month. I'd love to have you on my list!

And if you'd like to be notified whenever a book from my extensive backlist goes on sale for 99 cents or is offered for free for a limited time, be sure to follow me on Bookbub, and they'll send you an email alert on the day the book is discounted, so you won't miss out.

All for now, and happy reading!

Best wishes,
Julianne

Excerpt From

The COLOR of FOREVER

by Julianne MacLean

From USA Today *bestselling author Julianne MacLean comes the next instalment in her popular Color of Heaven Series, where people are affected by real life magic—and miracles that have the power to change everything they once believed about life and love.*

Recently divorced television reporter Katelyn Roberts has stopped believing in relationships that last forever, until a near-death experience during a cycling accident changes everything. When she miraculously survives unscathed, a deeply-buried memory leads her to the quaint, seaside town of Cape Elizabeth, Maine.

There, on the rugged, windswept coast of the Atlantic, she finds herself caught up in the secrets of a historic inn that somehow calls to her from the past. Is it possible that the key to her true destiny lies beneath all that she knows, as she explores the grand mansion and its property? Or that the great love she's always dreamed about is hidden in the alcoves of its past?

CHAPTER

One

I've often heard that a close brush with death can cause your life to flash before your eyes in an instant. There was a time I didn't believe it, because how could all the experiences of a person's life possibly replay in his or her mind in such a short interval? Wouldn't your brain be occupied by the task of finding a way to save yourself?

Some say that such a flashback is brought on by a rush of adrenaline, which causes the brain to function at hyper speed. Have you ever been in a situation of shock and panic, where the disaster appears to occur in slow motion before your eyes, yet you can do nothing about it? When your body simply cannot keep up with the velocity of your perceptions?

In other situations, people have been known to take action with incredible strength and speed—lifting a car, for instance, to save a crushed child. How can that possibly occur? Is adrenaline truly that powerful?

Others theorize that the purpose is to help the person to access all his memories in order to find a way to save himself, or someone else. This seems logical to me, but who knows the true origins of such miracles?

All I can tell you is that I believe it is true. Life *can* flash before your eyes at the moment of impending death. I know it because I am one of those people who—while skirting death by a narrow margin—experienced a rush of adrenaline so potent that I glimpsed my entire lifetime, like slides flashing rapidly before my eyes. So who am I to doubt such a phenomenon?

What I fail to understand, however, is why I saw a life that was completely different from my own.

Oddly, the life I viewed in those fleeting seconds before the accident was not someone 'else's. The memories were all mine. I was the so-called protagonist in the show, confused as to why I felt such a deep, emotional connection to the people in my mind's eye, who were complete strangers to me. I felt a love and a longing for them, with as much emotion and clarity as any other momentous experience, yet little that was revealed matched the existence I'd known.

In reality, on that day I peddled up the mountain with my cycling club, I was a thirty-two-year-old, childless divorcee. I wish I could say I was emotionally secure, happy to be a single, independent woman, and optimistic about starting a new chapter in my life. But on that particular day—like most days recently—I had woken up feeling desperately alone, with a knot in my belly the size of a football. And more so, because my ex-husband had just remarried after receiving a fantastic promotion. All I wanted to do was get into my car, drive to his office, ride the elevator up fourteen floors and rant to his boss about what a louse he was.

Did they not understand that he was unreliable, dishonorable and self-absorbed? How could they promote him to a partner in their firm when he was a philandering cheater who couldn't be faithful to his first wife?

It boggled my mind that Mark always won. No matter who he stepped on, or who paid the price in tears, he always got what he wanted, then slept like a baby each night after enjoying the fruits of his labors—the luxury home, the trips to Barbados, the Mercedes and the beautiful wife who lay beside him in bed—probably wearing Victoria's Secret lingerie.

At one time, I was that privileged, beautiful wife—and oh, how he adored me in those early years. I was an up-and-coming celebrity television journalist in Seattle with a good chance of eventually becoming anchor on the evening news. While still in my twenties, I covered major political events and attended charity dinners with the mayor. Meanwhile, Mark was an ambitious criminal lawyer who loved showing me off at every opportunity, because I shone a bright light on us as a stylish Seattle couple.

I hesitate to use the word perfect—because nothing is ever perfect, right?—but that's how it felt, and that's certainly how others perceived us. At least until everything came crashing down like a jet spinning out of the sky.

I remember, precisely, the day the turbulence began, and it's rather unnerving that I can pinpoint the exact moment.

Mark and I had gone out for dinner with a few friends,

and after they said goodnight and got into a cab, I stepped to the curb to flag down the next one, but Mark grabbed my arm and pulled me back.

"What are you doing?" he asked, glancing down the street. "It's barely midnight. Let's stay out."

My heart sank because it had been a busy week at work and I was ready for bed. Looking back on it, I'm sure I could have convinced him to head home by slipping my arms around his waist, smiling coquettishly and promising some fun and games in the bedroom, but as I mentioned, it had been a long week and I was spent. I wasn't in the mood for "sexy talk," so I said the absolute wrong thing with a tired sigh.

"Come on, Mark. We're not in college anymore. I'm done for the night. Besides, it's time to grow up. Let's leave the after-hours' partying to the twenty-somethings."

His head drew back and his eyebrows lifted. It was as if I had suggested we retire, downsize and move to Florida.

"You just want to go home? It's Friday night."

"I know…" I felt suddenly intimidated, inadequate. *Dull*. So I backpedaled and struggled to explain myself. "I'm sorry, but you know how stressful my week was. That story about the alcoholic bus driver really took its toll on me. I'm not up for more socializing. I just want to curl up on the sofa and watch TV."

Frustrated, he inhaled deeply and held his breath for a few seconds, then looked away, down the street again. "We watch TV every night, Katelyn. It's *Friday*. Don't you want to be a social butterfly?"

Maybe I was a tad irritable because it was late. Moreover, I loathed the fact that he wanted me to fake it and play a role, when I'd just explained how tired I was. I wished he felt the same way—that the idea of curling up on the sofa with me held at least *some* appeal.

I realized in that moment that for him, it was the worst kind of torture—to stay at home, just the two of us. Sure, there had been a time when I loved going out every weekend, but I was starting to grow away from that lifestyle. I preferred an early evening that didn't result in a pounding headache the next morning.

"Who are you hoping to see?" I asked. "The guys from work? Because I'm quite sure the partners are all at home with their wives and children. Isn't that what you aspire to? To take some time away from the rat race?"

He frowned. "What are you trying to say, Katelyn?"

I knew, by the challenging tone of his voice, that he knew exactly what I was trying to say. I'd been dropping hints for two years.

"Don't you think it's time we slowed down a little? I just turned thirty. You know I want to have kids, and if we're ever going to be parents, we can't be out partying till four in the morning every weekend."

He glanced around at the people walking past us on the sidewalk and lowered his voice. "I've told you, I'm not ready for that."

"So you've said. Many times."

I spoke loudly, heatedly, without concern for who might take notice, which was dangerous because, as I said earlier, we were recognizable in Seattle. Anyone could whip out a cell phone and start recording our argument. It could show up on YouTube within the hour.

Mark grabbed me by the arm and dragged me into the recessed doorway of a flower shop.

"I've been patient," I continued, roughly shaking his

hand off my arm, "waiting for you to be ready, but I'm not getting any younger and neither are you. If we don't start trying soon, I'm going to be popping out my first kid when I'm forty."

His eyes widened with horror. *"Forty!"*

I laughed at him, bitterly. "What...? You think we'll never be forty? We *will* be, eventually, Mark, and that day's not that far off. And guess what. We're going to be fifty someday, too. I'd like for our kids to at least be in middle school by then. Wouldn't you?"

He stared at me in disbelief for a moment, then raised his hand to stop me from saying anything more. "I don't want to talk about this right now."

"When *will* you want to talk about it?" I replied. "Because you always put it off. You change the subject. And for the record, I hate it when you put your hand in my face like that."

He turned away and strode to the curb. "Go home if you want, Katelyn. I'm staying out."

I scoffed resentfully, and followed him. He raised his arm to flag down a cab for me.

"Do you want this one?" he asked as it approached.

"Yes," I firmly replied. "I'm going home. Where are you going?"

He shrugged a shoulder and reached into his pocket for his phone. "I don't know yet. I need to see where people are." He searched through his texts.

I exhaled with defeat as the cab stopped in front of us. Suddenly, I wished the night weren't ending like this. We'd had such a great time at dinner, and Mark had been his most charming self. He sat next to me with his arm across the back of my chair, listening attentively as I talked about the bus driver story. And he was so impossibly handsome in that gray sweater I'd bought for him at Bergdorf Goodman, in New York. It matched his gray-blue eyes and made me remember why I'd fallen in love with him. *Was I crazy, leaving him like this, downtown at midnight on a Friday night?*

The cab driver waited until I opened the back door, but I hesitated before getting in. "Mark," I said more gently. "Why don't you come home with me? We can talk about this some more. Figure things out."

His eyes lifted briefly. "I told you, I don't want to talk about it tonight. Go home. Get in your pajamas. I'll see you later."

He returned his attention to his phone and began texting.

"Fine. Bye," I tersely said as I slid into the back seat and shut the cab door.

I watched him, still texting on the sidewalk as we drove off, but he never looked up. I wonder now if he had texted Mariah, the sexy, young articling clerk at his firm. I hadn't suspected anything at the time, but if I had known about her—known what she looked like and how all the men at the firm were drooling over her like schoolboys—might I have mustered the energy to stay out a few extra hours and suffer the headache the following morning?

Probably.

─◎─

Much later that night, Mark slipped quietly into bed, working hard not to wake me. I lay with my back to him and pretended to be asleep, though I was fully aware that it was past 3:00 a.m. and he smelled like cigarette smoke. I wondered where he had been, but didn't want to start another fight, so I decided to wait until the morning to ask about his night.

When I woke, he was gone. At least he'd left me a note on the kitchen table to let me know he'd risen early to hit the gym. It wasn't unusual for him to work out on Saturday mornings—even with a hangover—so I simply let it go. I didn't bring up our argument again.

Three weeks later, I would come to regret that decision.

Three

"**I** don't understand," I said as I followed Mark to the door where his suitcase was packed and waiting. "Maybe we hit a few rough patches lately, but I thought everything was fine. How can you just pack up and leave like this? Don't you even want to *try* to work things out?"

"Trust me. It's better this way," he replied as he reached hurriedly for his coat in the front hall closet. "There's no point dragging this out over months or even years."

"But…" I watched him slip his arms into the sleeves and check his pockets for his gloves. "You haven't even given me a chance to process this. I'm in shock, Mark. I come home from work and find you sitting on the sofa with your bags packed. Surely you're not serious. You're not going to leave right now."

"I am."

The chill in his tone made my stomach turn over with a sickening ball of dread. "How long have you been feeling this way?"

"A while," he replied, without hesitation, which came as a total shock to me.

"Wait…" I reached out to touch his harm, wanting to hold on to him. He was my husband and I loved him. We were supposed to be building a life together. I thought he was going to be the father of my children. "I know you weren't keen on the idea of having a baby," I said, "but we can talk about that. Maybe I've been pushing too hard lately. But I still don't understand how you suddenly decided, at the drop of a hat, to throw our entire marriage out the window."

"It's not at the drop of a hat," he replied irritably as he wrapped his Ralph Lauren scarf around his neck and bent to pick up his travel-sized suitcase. "I told you, I've been thinking about this for a while."

"But you never said anything." My heart began to thump heavily in my chest and perspiration beaded on my brow. *Was this really happening?* "I thought we were happy."

He rolled his eyes and shook his head, which caused a sudden rush of anger to thrash in my blood. I gritted my teeth, grabbed him roughly by the arm and forced him to look directly at me. "How long have you felt this way?"

He paused. "You and I both know it's gotten stale lately. A year maybe," he conceded at last.

I blinked a few times and spoke with rancor. "A year? And you think we're *stale*? What the hell does that mean?"

"It means we're not in love like we used to be. The spark's gone. Come on, Katelyn, there's no passion and you know it."

I let out a breath of shock. "No, I don't. I'm your wife and I was ready to have a baby with you. Now I find out that you're *not that into me?*"

This news was like a knife in my gut, because I'd always worked so hard to make Mark happy—to do all the things he enjoyed, like tennis and water skiing. I showed interest in his work and I was always supportive of what he wanted. I was never a nag and I never "let myself go," as far as appearances were concerned. I hadn't gained a single pound since the day we married, nor had I succumbed to the temptation of sweatpants, or wearing no makeup, or pulling my hair back in a ponytail on the weekends. I'd avoided all of that, for him.

"There's really no point in discussing this," he said, raising his hand in my face and turning away, moving toward the door. "It's over, Katelyn. There's nothing you can do to change it. It's better to make a clean, swift break, because I just don't want to be married anymore."

He opened the door and walked out, leaving me speechless and gasping in the front hall, unable to do anything but rush to the open doorway and stare as he drove away.

What I didn't know at the time was that he had driven straight to Mariah's apartment, where he'd already begun the paperwork for a legal separation. I received the documents not long after that.

OTHER BOOKS BY

JULIANNE MACLEAN

The American Heiress Series
To Marry the Duke
An Affair Most Wicked
My Own Private Hero
Love According to Lily
Portrait of a Lover
Surrender to a Scoundrel

The Pembroke Palace Series
In My Wildest Fantasies
The Mistress Diaries
When a Stranger Loves Me
Married By Midnight
A Kiss Before the Wedding – A Pembroke Palace Short Story
Seduced at Sunset

The Highlander Trilogy
The Rebel – A Highland Short Story
Captured by the Highlander
Claimed by the Highlander
Seduced by the Highlander
Return of the Highlander
Taken by the Highlander

The Royal Trilogy

Be My Prince
Princess in Love
The Prince's Bride

Dodge City Brides Trilogy

Mail Order Prairie Bride
Tempting the Marshal
Taken by the Cowboy – a Time Travel Romance

Colonial Romance

Adam's Promise

Contemporary Fiction

The Color of Heaven
The Color of Destiny
The Color of Hope
The Color of a Dream
The Color of a Memory
The Color of Love
The Color of the Season
The Color of Joy
The Color of Time
The Color of Forever
The Color of a Promise
The Color of a Christmas Miracle
The Color of a Silver Lining

About the Author

Julianne MacLean is a *USA Today* bestselling author of many historical romances, including The Highlander Series with St. Martin's Press and her popular American Heiress Series with Avon/Harper Collins. She also writes contemporary mainstream fiction, and The Color of Heaven was a *USA Today* bestseller. She is a three-time RITA finalist, and has won numerous awards, including the Booksellers' Best Award, the Book Buyer's Best Award, and a Reviewers' Choice Award from Romantic Times for Best Regency Historical of 2005. She lives in Nova Scotia with her husband and daughter, and is a dedicated member of Romance Writers of Atlantic Canada. Please visit Julianne's website for more information and to subscribe to her mailing list to stay informed about upcoming releases.

www.juliannemaclean.com

Made in the USA
Columbia, SC
03 March 2022